Only the Ocean

By Cecily Knobler

Published by Encore Press Inc, 2020

Cover design: Kinmond Smith, Smokin' Dogs Inc.

Editor: Wendy Morley

Previously published as Five Thousand Three Hundred Miles by Q&S Publishing, 2015

Encore Press Inc,
1-1675 Sismet Rd.,
Mississauga, ON
L4W 4K8
Canada

www.encore-press.com

Ordering Information:
Quantity sales. Special discounts are available on quantity purchases by corporations, associations, and others. For details, contact the publisher at the address above.

Contact available via website.

Published in Canada

ISBN: 978-1-989728-24-6
Electronic edition ISBN: 978-1-989728-25-3

"To all the Brits I've loved before..."

Chapter One:
Life Before Life

My name is Beth Wilton and my life is small. I live in a small town in central California, I drive a small car, I have small feet. I watch a lot of reality television and I'm usually asleep by 9:30pm. I know exactly what I'm going to pack for my work lunch every day (a tuna sandwich, some carrots and an orange juice). I usually lay my clothes out the night before. And I'm only 29 years old.

I like my small life, but 10 years ago I wasn't like this. When I was 19 I did Jell-O shots and keg-stands, and I danced in the streets on rainy nights. I laughed hard every day about something totally absurd. My heart was fully intact. But then one day, it cracked into more pieces than I thought a heart even had. And I wasn't even close to ready for it.

I had met Ben my freshman year at UC San Diego. He was tall, with flaxen blonde hair (yes, flaxen), hazel eyes and a laugh that brought me to my knees. All the girls in my dorm were enamored with him, especially when he'd come back from a surf meet, his hair casually messy, his wetsuit shiny and put to good use. Somehow, it was me he set his sights on, and this was thrilling.

I'd been chatting with my roommate Lisa in our tiny dorm room on the east quad when a thin envelope was shoved under the door. She grabbed it and said, "It has your name on it! What is it?" She handed it to me and I furiously tore it open and read it out loud. "It says,

'Beth, you are cordially invited to the Beta Theta Pi Fraternity Crush Party this Saturday at The Tavern. Come and find out which brother has a crush on you!'"

"I don't want to go to this," I'd said emphatically. "Those guys are crazy. Plus, I don't like surprises."

"Are you insane? You're going and you're gonna love it."

Saturday night I put on a silver miniskirt and a black silk top with flowing sleeves. Somehow Lisa convinced me to let her do my hair, and I had to admit, it looked hotter than usual. Lipstick? Check. Perfume sprayed once behind the ears? Of course. And even though I pretended to be cynical, my heart was wide open.

I got to the party late and immediately recognized a few guys and women from my dorm. I wasn't much of a drinker, but a glass of champagne wouldn't hurt. I'd only had a few sips before I was dragged out to the dance floor by a group of fun sorority girls. So this was college? Well in that case, maybe I could be one of those carefree girls who knew how to have the perfect amount of fun. It's not like I wouldn't go to class on Monday. I wasn't going to lose myself. It was just one dance, after all. Or four. Or possibly five.

I'd just been twirled into a glowing, wild, sexy fit of laughter when — it seemed like out of nowhere — Ben appeared beside me. I knew who he was, of course. We all did. But when he put his hand gently on the small of my back, I could tell this interaction would be special.

"So," he said, his voice sounding sweeter than I'd expected. "Did you figure out who has the crush on you?"

I laughed. "Um, is it that guy?" I pointed toward the bartender.

"No, not him."

"How about that dude?" I asked as I gestured toward another fraternity brother nearby.

"No, not him either," he whispered as he wrapped his arms around my waist from the back. "Turn around right now and you'll see him."

He loosened his grip just enough that I could wiggle around to face him. "Oh it's you!"

"Yes, it's me! I've wanted to ask you out since I first saw you in our political science class, but I didn't think someone like you would give me the time of day."

"Someone like me?"

"Yeah, you know, someone so beautiful and so oblivious to it. That's what makes you stand out. You don't even know how pretty you are."

Oh this guy was good. I laughed, "Yes, sure. I'm sure you have all kinds of problems getting women to like you."

He didn't argue the fact. Instead he said, "May I kiss you?"

Normally, I'd have said no. Even though at that time I had not experienced real romance, I had watched a lot of TV and wanted to be courted in the traditional sense like my favorite fictional characters were. But Ben's breath smelled of spearmint and gin. The room was dim and the music was invigorating. And I guess my body said yes without words, because the next thing I knew, his lips were on mine and the room froze.

Let me skip ahead now. Six months of being on Ben's arm and being in Ben's arms was unlike any feeling I'd ever had. I glided through the atmosphere like a happy ghost, one who'd fulfilled everything she'd set out to do in life. I didn't hear cars honking or the rattle of talking pundits on television. Anything that I normally found annoying was now muted by my pure adoration and, okay I'll say it — love — of this amazing, beautiful, charming man.

That feeling was abruptly terminated on one abnormally hot day in March when I walked into a café on campus and saw Ben kissing a tall blonde exchange student. I walked right up to him, hoping my eyes had deceived me. Unfortunately, they hadn't.

"Is that you?" I asked stupidly, disbelievingly … in retrospect, desperately.

"Beth!" Funnily enough, this was the first and only time I'd ever seen Ben startled.

And then I screamed what I'd assume any 18- or 19-year-old woman who was in the throes of a delusional love spiral would scream: "You said you loved me!"

I then fled, descending a short staircase, not unlike an especially dramatic Scarlett O'Hara. And believe me, just like Rhett Butler, Ben did not give a damn. Oh sure, he pretended to with phone calls and flowers. But after a couple of weeks of "She meant nothing to me, baby" and "It was just one kiss," he called to say we were through. After all that, he was the one who ended it. I thought I'd never breathe again. I'm not sure I have.

It wasn't so much that he had proclaimed to be in love with me, though he had. It was those quiet moments when he was touching me and telling me "You are so beautiful" with so much conviction that any doubt I may ever have had about my thighs or my hips or my nose completely melted out of my mind, like honey dripping from a hive.

One week later, he was openly dating the tall blonde woman and I briefly stopped going to class. It was as though I could not bridge the gap between the valves of my heart. I don't mean this metaphorically, like a cheap love song. It was a physical feeling, like the ventricles weren't properly pumping blood or air or whatever they're supposed to pump from one side to the other.

Ben was my first love, my first time having sex and my first heartbreak. And even though I did resume breathing, going to class again and even dancing a little, my heart sealed up that day and has never fully reopened. Everyone told me that time would heal it, but all time did was put gauze over my sadness. It was still there, but it just wasn't quite as focused anymore.

So now I'm 29 and I guess I'm okay. I go to work, I occasionally get set up on dates, I eat, I breathe. I have lots of great girlfriends and a sister, Riley, who's my best friend. Next week is my 30th birthday and I'll probably gather the girls for drinks and karaoke. (The two most definitely go hand in hand.) Like I said, my life is small and I wouldn't really know what to do with it if it grew any bigger.

****

At 7:00pm, I heard a rap, tap, tap on the door. Before I could even ask, I heard Riley's muffled voice yelling, "It's me, surprise! Let me in!"

I opened the door to find my sister with a bouquet of tulips and a small box. "Happy birthday!" she proclaimed.

"But my birthday is not for another five days!"

"True, but sisters get to give their presents first. And plus, I couldn't wait." She pulled me to the couch where she handed me the flowers and the box. "Here. Open!"

"Are you drunk?" I asked, half-jokingly. "These flowers are beautiful, thank you! I should find a vase…"

"Before you do, open the box."

"Jeez, bossy. Okay, okay." I tore off the light pink wrapping paper and opened the long box. "Is it a watch? What is this?" After removing the tissue paper, I saw a piece of paper. "Great, you got me an email."

"Read it, silly!"

I began, "This is to certify that Beth Wilton, sister of Riley Wilton, the most amazing sister in all the land, is now the proud owner of one airplane ticket and three nights in a posh hotel in London." I could literally feel my jaw drop. "Whoa, Riley!"

Riley hugged me tightly. "You have never treated yourself to a vacation and I know you've always wanted to go to London. You were never gonna bite the bullet, so I thought I'd do it for you. Plus, Mark gets so many airline miles, we don't even know what to do with them. I was able to use them for both the ticket and the hotel!"

"Does your husband know you've used his miles?"

"I'm telling you, he won't even notice. Beth, aren't you excited?"

My eyes welled up. "This is too much. I can't, I can't! Plus, I can't get off work, you know that."

"You've spent the last 10 years saying the word can't and frankly I can't hear it anymore. I knew you'd bring up the work thing, so I took the liberty of calling your boss."

"Riley, you'll get me fired!"

"You know I wouldn't do that. I asked if you had any vacation time coming up and she told me you had three weeks. So surely you can take four days off. And I knew you'd never take me up on it, so…"

"Riley…" I warned, nervously.

"I went ahead and booked your flight. Your boss knows when you'll be off. You leave a week from Monday!"

It finally sunk in. "I'm going to London? I'm going to London! Riley, you're amazing! Wait, you're going with me right?"

"I would love to, but this trip is just for you. It's good to travel alone. You get in touch with yourself. I remember the first time I backpacked across Europe… "

I stopped her and teased, "Oh no, I don't have to hear about your backpacking trip again."

"Ha, ha. Fine. But this will be so good for you. I love you and you deserve this. You work so hard and you never let yourself be truly happy."

"I'm happy. I know you worry and I thank you for it, but I promise I'm good now."

"I know you're good. But you deserve the moon. You deserve to feel ecstatic again."

I laughed. "Oh, well, no pressure."

"Now. do you have any booze? We need to start celebrating your birthday right now!"

I cracked open an old bottle of red and poured two glasses. "To London! And to the best sister in the world."

"Cheers!" We clinked glasses. And all of my worry and 10 years of stifled hope came billowing up, skipping stones in my stomach.

Chapter Two:
Across The Pond

It didn't take a weather app to know it would be cold in London in November. I packed my long red coat, two cashmere scarves and pretty much every cute outfit I've ever owned. Riley came over to help me then remove many of those items.

"You don't need 12 outfits for four days. Just make sure to bring at least one sexy black dress and the rest should be warm and practical sweaters and stuff. And condoms."

"Riley! No. Gross. I'm not going to need condoms."

"Never say never," she insisted as she tossed a handful of Trojans into my suitcase.

"Well, at least hide them. I don't want airport security rifling through my things and thinking I'm a floozy."

"If you keep using words like floozy, they'll think you time traveled from the 50s."

"I feel like I did sometimes."

"You've got your passport and all your other info, right? Hotel?"

"I'm not seven! I've got everything. I still can't believe you did this for me. I don't know how to ever repay you."

"You can repay me by having a great time. How's that? Now hurry up, we've got to leave for the airport in an hour!"

About six hours into my window-seated flight and after two gin and tonics, a tea and an in-flight romantic-comedy, I drifted off to sleep. I immediately began having anxiety dreams. First I dreamt about losing my passport. Then my slumber-movies morphed into a seemingly never-ending search for the right English cobblestone street where my hotel room awaited. Every road led back to the same loop, with a man in a top hat pointing and saying, "You're going the wrong way. Beth, you're going the wrong way." I'd have this dream, waken with a start and wipe the adorable drool from the corners of my mouth, only to fall asleep and dream it again. It didn't take Freud to figure out the meaning of this, but I chalked it up to travel jitters.

Luckily, the middle seat was empty and the woman on the aisle was what I'd assume to be very English: polite and quiet. She sat crocheting a blanket and, incredibly apologetically, asked for Earl Grey tea from the flight attendants a few times. I'm also pretty sure I heard one of the English flight attendants apologize for serving her a tea. All this lovely self-awareness seemed like a perfect fit for my quiet, little life.

We landed at Heathrow a little after 8:00am and after what seemed like a year in customs, I hopped the Heathrow Express to Paddington Station, where I hailed a cab. Once I was outside, I couldn't believe how green everything was, fresh from a crisp November rain. Even though it was still morning, the sky was sepia toned, the pavement gold. Yes, there was a glittery bustle about the whole place, but a bustle unlike anything I'd ever seen in America. It was alive, but alive with history.

I'd dreamt of standing in this town my whole life and I was finally here. Everything back in the States — work, Ben, karaoke, my rigid routines — all of it seemed like it was on another planet, orbiting an entirely different sun. Maybe it was the jet lag, or maybe just my early-onset existential angst, but I honestly considered the idea that I'd entered some kind of parallel universe through a wormhole. All of these thoughts were probably caused by exhaustion, but it was surreal and dreamy and so I went with it.

"Where to, madam?" the older cabbie asked.

I didn't know! I dug around in my oversized purse to find the crumpled-up itinerary that Riley had written for me. She'd told me the hotel she booked was amazing, but I hadn't looked it up because I wanted it to be a surprise. "Oh sorry. We're going to the Savoy Hotel? On the Strand?"

"Excellent. That's a lovely choice!"

"Is it? I've never been; my sister booked it for me." I had a habit of telling people too much unsolicited information. Very American.

"That is some sister you have there, milady!"

"Yes, it was a birthday gift. So, what should I do while I'm here? Obviously, I'll go do a little sightseeing, but what are some inside tips on the best restaurants or pubs or…"

He cut me off. "I think it's best to explore these things for yourself. Sure, I could tell you my favorite curry restaurant or a popular nightclub, but it's more fun when you happen upon things you love. Then they become yours."

"I like that. Yes, I want to find some things and make them mine."

"You're in the right city."

I rested my head on the window and must have dozed off for a bit because when I woke, I heard the cabbie gently say, "We've arrived madam. That's 12 pounds."

I looked up to see the most exquisite and unique hotel. We'd entered an alcove and there was a green, neon sign that read "Savoy." Men in top hats and tails rushed over to open the cab door. "Will we have the pleasure of your stay?"

"Yes! I'm staying here!" I exclaimed as if I couldn't quite believe it myself.

"Excellent. It would be my pleasure to assist you with your bags." He lugged my ridiculously large suitcase into the lobby and I gave him a pound. I wanted to ask him everything about his life, just because he had an English accent. The same went for the cabbie, the gentleman in customs and the lady who took my train ticket. I wanted to follow every single person I came across on Instagram, but I decided to tone down my need to connect, if only for a moment.

"You're staying on the fifth floor. Please do let us know if there's anything we can do to make your stay lovelier," the woman at the front desk said as she handed me my room key.

Out of possible delirium, I almost replied, "What's your Instagram name? I'm going to follow you." Thankfully, I refrained.

My room was huge, covered in yellow and cream drapes, bedding and cashmere throw blankets. The king-sized bed had a soft gray tufted headboard and everywhere I looked was the most beautiful curved, oak furniture. But the bathroom! Everything was marble, from the floors to the walls. On the side of the tub was a gold button that said "Butler." Did I deserve this much luxury? Would I ever leave this room?

I noticed a kettle and immediately made myself a cup of English Breakfast while drawing a bath. Yes, this was all a waking dream and I planned to swim through its brilliance with my eyes wide open. A cup of tea, a bath and just a quick nap before my English adventure — and quite possibly my life — would begin.

Chapter Three:
Tuesday Night

When I woke from my nap, it was already 7:30pm. Just in time for dinner, I thought, even though I was delirious with jet lag. Since I wanted to get lost, I gave myself a no-cell-phone policy. Sure, I had one I'd keep in the room so I could occasionally check emails, but I wanted to make a concerted effort to be fully present everywhere I was. That meant no Candy Crush, no texting with friends and no Twitter surfing. I would show up 100 percent wherever I was, so that I'd never look back and think, "Gee, wish I'd actually been there when I was there."

As suspected, London was freezing. I layered some clothes, wrapped my favorite scarf around my neck and headed down to the lobby. I decided to take the cabbie's advice and go on a real adventure. I didn't ask the concierge or the doorman where to go, because then it would be their trip, not mine. I headed outside, closed my eyes for a second and then in a quick decision, turned left.

After a few blocks, I stumbled upon a red-bricked pub/eatery called The Spotted Pig. Perfect. After a basket of fish & chips and a pint of Guinness at the bar, I began to think I should head back as I was getting increasingly exhausted. Until …

"Excuse me, I couldn't help but notice you have the smallest hands. They're so wee. You're so very, very wee." A man with reddish blonde hair and the iciest blue eyes I'd ever seen suddenly appeared on the barstool next to me. "I'm Liam."

He was sitting so close that I automatically became insecure. Did I have ketchup on my lips? Had my rosy perfume worn off? I outstretched my hand awkwardly. "Hi, I'm Beth."

"An American," he said with a slight slur. "What fun!" I heard a tiny lilt in his voice, not quite English. "I don't usually make it a point to walk up to strangers, but you just looked so alone and pretty."

"Ah, you're too kind," I said, excited but with trepidation.

"I just can't get enough of your accent. It's brilliant." He then slowed down his speech to do his best American impression. "Iiiim from Ala-Baaaam-a. I tawk like thiiiiis."

"First of all, that's the worst impression I've ever heard. What was that? Also, I'm not from Alabama. I'm from California. What's your accent, by the way? I can't quite place it."

"Can't place it?" He flirtatiously touched my hand. "Do these hints help? St. Patrick? Luck of the 'blank'?"

"You're Irish!"

"I'm Irish! Not sure what gave it away. My red hair, my accent or the fact that I'm a little toasted."

"Are you? What are you drinking?"

"I've been drinking whiskey tonight. Could I get you one?"

"When in Rome, I guess? Sure, thank you!"

He somewhat politely motioned the bartender over and ordered two shots of Jameson. They seemed familiar with one another. "What brings you here, Miss American?"

"I'm actually on my first vacation to London, if you can believe it."

"Welcome to our fair city! Well, I say 'our' but I'm actually from Dublin originally." The bartender placed two thick shots in front of us. "We need to make a toast in your honor."

We each raised our glasses. "Do your worst, sir!"

"May you be 30 minutes in heaven before the devil knows you're dead."

It wasn't quite as poetic as I'd hoped, but I took the shot anyway. I'd literally spoken to this man for less than five minutes, so my hopes for something sweet were probably misplaced.

"Good girl. Want another?"

"I'd better not, actually. I've really enjoyed this, but I'm so very tired."

"You can't possibly be thinking about leaving this pub, can you? How long are you in London?"

"Only three nights. And if I spend tomorrow hungover in my room, my first day will be wasted!"

"Well maybe you'll allow me to show you around town tomorrow? I know you don't know me, but I assure you I'm not a serial killer."

What luck I was having! I'd met a very cute blue-eyed Irishman on my first venture out and he wanted to show me the town. Best part? He wasn't a serial killer! What idiot would say no to this? "That sounds nice. How 'bout I meet you here tomorrow. Say 1:00pm?"

"Sounds great. You'll be here, right? Should we exchange mobile numbers?"

"I'm not doing the cell thing while I'm here. But don't worry, I'll be here at 1:00."

"You're not doing the cell thing, but are you doing this?" In a split second, without notice, without permission, he leaned in and kissed me. His lips were dry, but soft. The kiss was sharp and confident and reeked of sexy danger.

"Well, I guess I am doing that it turns out. But next time, ask."

"Oh, so they'll be another kiss, then?"

"We'll see how I feel tomorrow," I said coyly. "Good night, Liam." I stood up.

"Good night, Miss American. I'll see you then."

I walked back to the hotel feeling strange. And pretty. And like I was having one of those dreams where nothing made sense, but I was okay with it.

Chapter Four:
Wednesday

My internal clock was completely off so I woke up in my luxurious Savoy sheets every two hours. I finally got out of bed at 11:00am and lounged in my cream, silk robe while watching BBC television. I drank tea and stared out the window at the Thames River. It was all so gray and glittery and established. Kings and queens had stared at this river. And quite possibly David Bowie.

At noon I showered and put on cute skinny jeans with a close-fitted Angora sweater. Not too tight, of course. We didn't want to give Liam the wrong idea. I wrestled with whether to arrive early or late to the pub, and landed on leaving the hotel right at 1:00 for a 1:05 arrival. Late, but certainly not insulting.

I walked in and the restaurant was completely and utterly bare, with the exception of an older woman tending bar. "Hello," she said. "Have a seat wherever you'd like. Our lunch specials are on the chalkboard."

"Oh, I'm actually meeting someone here. I'll just sit at the bar if that's okay."

"It most certainly is. May I get you anything?"

It seemed too early for a cocktail. "Perhaps just a cup of coffee?"

"Coming right up!"

I checked my watch. It was 1:08 and no Liam. The bartender served me my coffee, which was way too European and black and strong. "Might I trouble you for some cream and sugar?"

"Oh of course," she said. I was hoping she'd follow that up with something about how American I was for needing my coffee sweet. But she didn't mention it.

I let the caffeine seep in, but the buzz was rather jarring. Watch check: 1:23. This was ridiculous. I hadn't come all this way to be stood up by a stranger. "I will not take it personally. I will not take it personally," I inwardly chanted. At 1:35, I had finished my coffee and asked for the tab. "Oh well," I'd said to the polite barkeep. "I guess my new friend isn't coming."

"Good riddance to that friend!" she said supportively.

Scarf back on and out the door I went. I had a lot of sightseeing to do anyway so I headed in the direction of the Tube station in the hopes of making it to the Tower of London. Just as I was about to venture down the Tube stairs, I heard, "Hey, American girl! Wait!"

I turned to see Liam walking briskly toward me. His eyes looked even bluer than the night before and he was carrying a pink rose.

"I'm so sorry I was late. The train broke down at King's Cross and I couldn't afford to hire an Uber. Please, will you ever forgive me?"

"Of course. I'm going to the Tower of London. Would you like to join?"

"Off with our heads!" he yelled.

"Is that a yes?"

He grabbed my hand. "There is no other torture chamber I'd rather be in with you."

We ran down the steps and I could smell his soap, and his cigarettes. Since I'd resigned myself to spending the day alone, I was both intrigued and put out by his sudden presence. I'd always been someone who needed to have a plan, so when that suddenly changed, it took my neurosis a minute to catch up.

He held my hand on the Tube as we listened to a street performer play a sweet ballad on his guitar. We talked about light things: the weather, his job as an electronics store clerk, our favorite bands. He was cute in that inaccessible way a foreigner is cute. You almost wonder if you're the same species.

We strolled through the Tower property, listening to the tour guide. When we got to the Crown Jewels, my blood rushed. They glowed red, purple and silver in a way those colors had never appeared to me before. Liam didn't seem especially moved by them, often commenting at how gaudy and over-indulgent the English were. "Careful," I warned, "or I'll have you locked up."

"You can lock me up anytime you please. Do you want to find a bathroom we can make out in?" His Irish lilt was so playful and sexy, but I wasn't sure if he was serious.

"I think I'm good for now. Maybe at Buckingham Palace if the prince will allow?"

"You want to go there too?"

"Today is my sightseeing day! I need to see it all. But I completely understand if that's not your bag. It's all good." I didn't usually sound so hippie-like. I was trying it on as a persona and didn't totally hate it.

"As long as there's a pay off!"

I wasn't quite sure what he meant by that, but I laughed anyway. "We don't have a lot of light left. I want to get an Abbey Road crossing in too."

We scurried around town to catch as much of the must-sees as we could. Well, I caught them, he mostly texted on his phone or stared at me. By the time we hit dusk, he proposed we go to dinner.

"Sure. You're such a fantastic tour guide."

"I deserve a kiss now."

This should have seemed endearing. A blue-eyed, dimpled Irishman who devoted his day to accompanying a Yank stranger. But somehow it wasn't endearing. It seemed forced and slightly aggressive.

"Oh Liam, is that all you think about?" I joked.

"When in your company, yes it is. Let's go get food and a drink back on the Strand. You're staying near there, aren't you?"

Although I wanted to be alone, I was holding the pink rose he'd given me and it seemed awfully rude to ditch him now. One drink won't hurt, I decided, although I made it a point to not mention my hotel by name.

Once we were back near the Spotted Pig, Liam pointed to a different brick restaurant/pub and said, "Let's go there. They make a strong Jack and Coke." He led me in and ordered from the bar before we'd even sat down. I got a pint of Harp beer and started to feel a bit anxious as we sat down in a red leather booth. "Well, American friend, should we get some bangers and mash?"

"Do you keep calling me American friend or Miss American because you don't remember my name?"

"Don't be silly!"

"What's my name?" I plodded.

"It's Christy. Or Jennifer."

The whole thing had become so surreal that I was no longer in the mood to play along. "No, crazypants, it's Beth."

"Beth! Yes. I knew that. I'll admit I had forgotten for a moment, but my blood sugar is down. It makes me forgetful."

I laughed. "Oh is that a side effect?"

"It is. One way I can get it back up is to eat. Or drink. Or kiss you."

He was sitting across from me in the booth and it looked like he was about to get up to come over to my side, when the waitress came over to take our order. Liam seemed annoyed. Without asking me, he answered, "We'll just have a bowl of crisps if you've got 'em."

"You just want a snack?"

"Yes, for now." He looked at me. "Is that okay?"

It was actually preferable. I did not plan to stay for long. "Sure."

Liam was on his third drink by the time our appetizers came out. He was slurring just a bit and I wondered how I was going to excuse myself. He stood up, drink in hand, and asked me to slide over in my booth. "I'd like to sit by the American please."

"It's a bit tight on this side, don't you think?"

"I hope so," he said as he leaned in, Jack Daniels first, lips second and planted another unsolicited kiss on my lips.

I wish I wanted to have fun with his mouth. I wish I wanted to kiss him back in a carefree, "it was just my birthday and I'm in London" kind of devil-may-care way. Just me, with my tiny, soft life and him, with his Irish blue eyes. But it all just felt so wrong. Suddenly, a wave of sadness came over me and, even though it was not in my nature, I felt a need to be saved from his danger. Was this what awaited me? In my fantasies, I never needed to be saved, but the idea of a knight in shining armor was intriguing.

"Liam, I'm so beat. I think I'm still jet-lagged. Today was an absolute blast but I think it's time I turn in and call it a night."

"No! Please American, I mean Beth. I spent the whole day with you. Now you should spend the whole night with me."

"I didn't know we were doing a tit-for-tat kinda thing, but I have to go." I dug in my purse for 10 pounds, which I put on the table. "This should cover my drink. Thank you, Liam, for a lovely day."

I stood up, hugged him, and walked out the door. He followed me.

"Come on, please. I just need to feel your lips." He touched my arm, not terribly aggressively, but hard enough that I felt unsettled.

I continued in my attempt at levity. "I'll bet there are at least eight other cute American girls in there that you can make out with."

He grabbed my shoulder, this time rougher. "Beth, you're being very rude. I've gone out of my way for you today." His hand slid down to my wrist, which he held onto tightly. "Don't act like I'm going to hurt you. I'm not that guy. I just like you is all and I want you to hang out with me just a little longer."

Now I was scared. "Liam, let go. Enough is enough."

And just as he let go of my wrist to put his hands around my waist, I heard a gentle voice behind me. "Excuse me, mate. The woman asked you to let her go."

I turned around to see a man with sandy brown hair and wide-set greenish blue eyes. He was tall, or at least seemed tall, and he was dressed in that English mod way (ironically preppy, skinny jeans, skinny tie, scarf, Converse shoes.) My first thought was that I didn't need a new prince to save me from the old one. I just wanted to stop making bad decisions. I just wanted to sit still in my beautiful hotel room in this lovely city, whose inhabitants were becoming increasingly unpredictable.

Liam turned his body toward the man. "This is none of your business. We're fine. Why are you all so dramatic?"

The Englishman replied, "It appears to me that you are the one who is dramatic. And highly inappropriate. I suggest you leave or I'll make you wish you had." His accent was very posh-sounding. Like the King. Or a hoity toity BBC announcer.

I backed up, fully expecting Liam to make a scene or throw a punch. Surprisingly, he said, "None of this is worth it. Thanks for nothing, American girl." He stumbled back inside, his forehead sweaty, his breath swimming in alcohol.

I breathed a sigh of relief. "Thank you so much. I actually have no idea how I got myself into that mess."

"Are you okay? Did he hurt you?"

"No, I'm fine. I just feel so stupid."

"He was the stupid one, that's for sure." He said this with so much sincerity, I took a moment to absorb him. While I was intrigued by the large space between his pretty round eyes, I wasn't about to make the same mistake again. What did I think this trip was, a reality dating show? My boy-craziness was getting downright tacky. Get it together, Beth. Go back to the hotel, go to sleep.

He continued, "I'm Jack."

"Beth." I extended my hand, which he shook, creating an undeniably electric charge. And I don't just mean poetically. Or a static cling shock. It was as if the electrons in my atoms had reversed with the protons, creating a kind of antimatter effect. We were no longer governed by the laws of physics. We were bouncing around on a quantum level and I didn't even know it yet. I'm aware that description seems nonsensical, but so was this spark. "Well, Jack, thank you again. I should probably head back. I'm visiting and, well, I don't have much time here."

Politely, he said, "Of course. My goodness, you've had quite the night." He paused. "I will say it would be a real shame if you let the evening fade into oblivion with that person as a London representative. He in no way should be considered an ambassador to our city."

"Do you always talk like a politician?" I asked, slyly.

"I suppose … well I suppose I do! So sorry."

His kindness seemed to be a sweet remedy for Liam's chaos. But again, I told myself to cut it out. This guy rescues me from Liam? Was there going to then be a Scottish man with bagpipes to rescue me from the English dude? Would that line of "rescuers" go on forever until they blurred together in a primordial soup of Y-chromosomes and testosterone? Or could I just learn from my mistakes and get a good night's sleep?

I clutched my purse. "Thank you again. It was really cool of you to help me."

"My pleasure. By the way, do you like The Beatles?"

"Of course. Who would say no to that question?"

"Morons. Probably that bloke who was just out here. Well, anyway, my friend's Beatles cover band is playing soon, not too far from here. Would you be interested in going?" There was that spark again. I felt it in my ankles. Off my slight hesitation, he said, "Honestly, what could possibly be more English than bad Beatles covers?"

"That's an excellent question. I can't think of anything." For that matter, I also couldn't think of any reason not to go. "Is it walking distance?"

"Just two blocks. Does that mean you'll come?"

"Sure, okay. But I may not stay long."

"Excellent." He began charmingly tripping over his words as we strolled toward the bar. "Not the part about you not staying long, although I totally understand that decision if it should arise. Sorry, I'm babbling. You make me a bit nervous and I can't quite figure out why. You're very pretty, Beth. Obviously, I know nothing about you and you must think the men here are insane."

"I will say I'm a little surprised. I'd heard that Brits very rarely approached people they didn't know."

"It's true. I'm an exception. And that other bloke seemed to be Irish and they're not usually as reserved as we are. Or at all."

"Let's forget about him, please. It was a terrible error in judgment."

"Excellent idea. Well, alright." He pointed to a red, velvet rope outside of a small pub. "This is actually the venue. My friend said no need to queue up. We're on the list!"

"Oh we are, are we? How did he know you'd randomly meet a damsel in distress?"

"I've said we, when I meant me. It was just supposed to be me alone. But I'm quite glad that's not the case now."

He seemed too handsome to be so egoless. But maybe this was just the English way. "Let's do it!"

Jack gave his name to the doorman, who promptly ushered us inside. It was a beautiful space. Old cherry wood surrounded plush, black velvet couches. In the back of the room was a raised stage with white lights surrounding it. A beautiful, dark-haired woman immediately came over carrying a tray and asked us if we'd like champagne.

Jack looked at me. "I'll have some if you will."

"That sounds delicious, thank you." I carefully took a glass from the tray and handed it to Jack. Then, adorably, he took another one from the tray and handed it to me. We thanked the waitress and then both instinctively raised our glasses toward one another. "Cheers! To…um, to Jack and Beth, total strangers." I revised it. "To one nice stranger helping a silly foreigner get away from a not-so-nice stranger."

"To Jack and Beth," he said and we both took sips of the gold bubbles. Usually, a moment like that feels contrived. How could it not? We don't know one another and we've just toasted ourselves as if we were an item. Jack and Beth. Beth and Jack. I guess our celebrity couple name would be Jeth. Or Back. Hmmm. Celebrity names aside, it didn't feel contrived. It felt nice.

He asked me where I was from and I decided since this portion of the night seemed to be going so well, I wouldn't be the "one who discloses everything" woman. I'd just tell him the basics. "I'm from the States. How 'bout you? Were you born here?"

"I was born at Stratford-upon-Avon."

"Wasn't that Shakespeare's home?"

"William Shakespeare was my great, great, great-times-eight grandfather."

"Wow! Was he really?"

"No," he said dryly. "But it sounds nice, doesn't it?"

Uh oh, he was funny too. My old insecurities were chomping at the bit to be heard, jumping up and down like a third grader trying to get her teacher's attention. I pushed a strand of my mousy brown hair out of my eyes and smiled. "Yes, that does sound nice."

A short, rotund man took the stage and asked that the crowd "quiet down." There were only about 12 of us, all speaking in relatively hushed tones, so I laughed and asked Jack, "How much quieter can we get?"

Jack winked and said, "The man said to be quiet so please pipe down."

"Just curious, what was the point of the whole red velvet rope outside? There's no one here."

"It's Wednesday at 10:30 and this is a Beatles cover band full of late 30-somethings. I think the crowd representation is quite right."

"Fair enough!" We re-clinked our glasses. "How do you know this band, anyway?"

"The drummer, Ringo, if you will, used to be my dorm-mate at university."

The man on stage yelled, "So without further ado, please welcome to the stage, the one, the only, The Strawberry Fields!"

I squinted my eyes to see four almost middle-aged men as they took the stage. They were all wearing St. Pepper's outfits and Beatles wigs. Almost immediately, the unmistakable opening riff of "Come Together" filled the room. They were actually quite good. Not "Beatles" good, but good. "Nice," I shouted slightly over the music.

"It's wonderfully horrid, isn't it?"

"I actually think they're pretty good."

Jack smiled and put his hand ever so gently on the small of my back. It was light and non-invasive and yet still, I could feel my body soften. That electrical charge was palpable and it wasn't just my boy-craziness. At least I didn't think it was.

The band played a few more songs and then their "Paul" took center stage, as the white lights turned to blue. He began to sing "For No One" and I tapped into the saddest, sweetest memories. Jack smiled sweetly as my eyes watered. "The day breaks, my mind aches," the singer crooned and for the first time in years, I felt like I was standing in the exact spot at the exact time in which I was supposed to.

After a very exciting encore song and a somewhat tragic "Ringo" drum solo, the show ended. It was late and there were only eight or nine people left in the audience, including Jack and me. We nodded politely to the other couple, who appeared to be in their 60s. A silver-haired man leaned over and said "George Harrison, well, his name is Ian, is our son."

Jack replied, "Well both your son and George Harrison are commendable. Well done, you."

The band members then appeared at the bar, now wearing their regular modern clothes — t-shirts and jeans, mostly. Jack's "Ringo" friend had on a tweed blazer as well. We showered them with compliments and even though the bar was technically closed, Ringo convinced the bartender to give us one more round of champagne. I opted not to drink mine, as I was perfectly content in my semi-sobriety. In fact, I couldn't tell if my light buzz was from the drinks I'd had earlier in the evening, or the spark — that spark I couldn't ignore when Jack smiled out of the corner of his mouth.

I knew I didn't need to fill every emotional void with the arms of a man. And yet I didn't want to leave Jack's side. I was torn between holding his hand and standing alone, the latter a choice I'd always believed to represent strength and self-actualization. And as my mind tingled with this ridiculous self-imposed dilemma, Jack touched my hand with his and they folded into each other like origami.

"Is that all right?" he asked gently.

"It is." I didn't even have the sensation of forming those words in my head or on my lips. They just appeared in the air carried by sound waves that I didn't conjure.

We walked out of the club onto the gold, rainy street and suddenly I had a fear that Jack, despite being Jack, was going to turn into another Liam. "You saved my night, but I should probably get back to the hotel now."

"I'll walk you."

I was a little unsure as to where we were in relation to the Savoy. And while I trusted him, at least partly, I didn't want him to know where I was staying. These boys were getting tougher and tougher to judge. "I think I'm just gonna take a cab. You can help me flag one down, if you don't mind?"

"Of course, not a problem at all." He was so English. If he felt disappointment in the slightest, he wasn't letting on. Stiff upper lip and all that. "Here we go!" He waved a black cab over.

"Well, this has been lovely, Jack. I had…I had such a great time with you this evening. Thank you for introducing me to the Strawberry Fields! They're my new favorite cover band."

The taxi driver scowled and turned on his meter.

Jack laughed. "You have been the highlight of my year. Wait, that's too much. I shouldn't have said that."

"You're delightful." I hugged him tightly and quickly got into the cab. Just as the cabbie was about to hit the gas pedal, Jack tapped lightly on the window. "Sir could you wait just a second?" I asked the driver and rolled the window down.

"I…I…bollocks…the meter is running. It's just that I… well, I've not met anyone quite as sparkling, no, bright as you in a long time, or really, maybe ever. And I realize I'm not making sense and we do have a time limit here, but would you, maybe like to perhaps, if you're not too busy, like to get a cup of tea tomorrow?"

This felt so different from Liam's confident proposal. What kind of fool would say no to tea with Jack? Certainly not me. I turned to the cabbie. "Sorry about this."

"It's your money ma'am," he answered matter-of-factly.

Back to Jack, I replied the only way my brain would let me. "Yes. I would love to have tea with you tomorrow."

"Excellent. Can you meet me, erm … " He looked around the area. "How about at that very tea shop there. It's called the Prince Café. We're on Bow Street in case you forget. Should you write it down?"

"I never forget anything, I promise. What time?"

"Well traditionally, we'd meet at four. But I fear that's too late in the day. Does noon work? I'm going to take the day off tomorrow."

"I didn't even ask you what you did for a living. How rude of me!"

At this point, the driver cleared his throat. "You're already up to two pounds, ma'am."

Jack dug into his pocket and pulled out a 10-pound note. He gave it to the driver. "Here, please use this for payment." To me, he said, "I'm a barrister but it's awfully boring. Noon tomorrow at Prince Café on Bow Street? Sorry, I'm a worrier when it comes to plans."

"I will be there, I promise. Good night, Jack."

"Good night, Beth. See you tomorrow."

The cab pulled away and drove me two blocks to the Savoy. In a twist, my body felt light, but my spirit felt grounded. Something was very right here.

****

By the time I got into my beautiful room, it was close to 1:00am. I was shattered with exhaustion, but of course had to call Riley. I'd gotten a calling card before I left and put exactly 30 minutes on it. I figured that was enough time to check in, but not get too engrossed in conversations with people back in the States, no matter how much I missed them.

It rang three times until she answered. "Hey, I'm at work. Is everything okay?"

"Oh yeah, it's the afternoon there! What year is it?"

"Very funny. You know it's 1850. How is London? I noticed you haven't been tweeting one bit!"

"I've been very anti cell-phone. I want to try to be in the moment. It's only a few days."

"So is it amazing?"

"This city is incredible. And the hotel! I never want to leave it!"

"Have you? Left it?"

"Of course. In fact, I'm calling because I met two guys!"

Riley gasped. "Two? In what, two days? You are a floozy!"

"Nice call back. Well one of the guys was a total nitwit. His name was Liam and he got really handsy. So forget about him. But the other's name is Jack. And Riley? He's amazing. I know, I tend to crush hard, but honestly, this feels different. He's incredible."

"Actually, Beth, you don't really crush hard. The last time you did was in college and the rest have just been fillers. I love that you're feeling something! Tell me about him."

"He's tall. And a great dresser. And his voice is so sexy. And he's kind, as far as I can tell. He made me laugh. And there's this buzz I get around him. I've never felt that before."

"Is he a good kisser?"

"I don't know yet! That's the craziest part. The buzz came without making out or anything. It was just like…this feeling. Like we sparked."

"I love it! And yes, ma'am, would you be interested in one of our vacation packages?"

"What? Oh wait, did your boss just walk in?"

"Yes. So I can put you down for one of our 50,000-dollar upgrades?"

"Fifty thousand? What, do you think I'm poor? Put me down for the billion-dollar vacation package."

"Very well then ma'am. I'll be emailing you the paperwork." She then whispered. "I'll talk to you later. Have so much fun!"

"I love you!" We hung up and I crawled into bed. Jack's face swam into the neurons of my brain as I drifted off to sleep, eager for another day of London.

Chapter Five:
Thursday

After the first good night's sleep I'd had in days, I woke up at 10:00am with a glow. Oddly, I didn't have the urge to get all spruced up. A T-shirt, a V-neck sweater, a light jacket, some jeans, some boots. I didn't have the kind of supermodel hair you could just roll out of bed with, but I decided I'd skip a blow-out, as it had been raining/sleeting on and off since I'd gotten here. I would just be Beth. Beth with a little bit of shiny, pink lip-gloss and okay, a dash of under-eye concealer for my jet-lagged eyes.

My heart felt itchy and thin in all the best ways. I let the thought that today was similar to the Liam situation enter my mind and then I talked myself out of it. Yes, in both cases I met men in London who then invited me to a beverage the next day. But that's where the similarities ended. Liam had been forceful and cocky and drunk. I'd sat on the fence of adventure with him, never quite wanting to swing over to the other side.

Jack, on the other hand was…wow. There was a strong presence about him, yet being around him felt soft and lovely and safe. It was, of course, too soon to judge his character, but he had this way about him that made me feel like I'd known him my whole life. Like he'd been that pal in my Biology class who flirted by reminding me we had a quiz the next day. I could see him having my back.

"Beth!" I inwardly screamed. "Calm way down! You're in London, so go have some tea with this cool guy and if anything feels wrong, be prepared to walk away. You came to this enchanted place alone, you're gonna leave alone too. Breathe. Breathe, Beth."

I took a deep breath, grabbed my purse and umbrella and headed to Bow Street.

****

I arrived exactly at noon to find Jack sitting at a small, quaint table facing the door. He was wearing an argyle sweater and the coolest blue kicks I'd ever seen on a man. His smile lit up the block. Be cool, Beth. He stood up when I arrived.

"Hi Jack! Am I late? Sorry if I'm late!"

"You're becoming like a true English lady. We apologize when we've done nothing wrong."

"Oh sorry. I mean, I'm not sorry. I'm…shit."

He laughed. "May I take your coat?"

I, unfamiliar with this custom, awkwardly stuck my arms out facing him. He gently tugged on the coat sleeves and then finally asked that I turn around. "Thank you," I said, my breath light.

He pulled a chair out for me and I sat down. A tall male waiter came over immediately and asked if we'd like to order.

Jack asked me, "Do you have any special kind of tea in mind?"

"I'll let you pick as I'm, you know, kind of a coffee person mostly."

"I know just the thing." He turned to the waiter. "Please, may we have a nice African Red tea? And actually, if it's not too much trouble, could we get the cheese, cucumber sandwich and crumpets platter?" He turned back to me. "Is that alright? Are you allergic to cheese? Or deliciousness?"

"I'm not allergic to anything! Although did you really just say cheese, and cucumbers?"

"I did. You're going to love it!"

And I did. Over the next hour and a half, we drank the richest, creamiest tea and ate cute little crust-free sandwiches and crumpets. Twice, we both reached for a crumpet at the same time, our fingers softly brushing one another's, that electricity buzzing around us. The more he talked or listened, the more I wanted to hear him talk or know that he listened.

We talked about our friends and favorite movies and cities. His eyes, which now appeared to be beautifully gray-green to catch the fibers of his sweater, lit up when he talked about people and places he loved. We'd find ourselves often saying the same words at the same time and then laughing with that knowing "I see you" kind of smile that bonds two strangers in a split second.

The check came and Jack paid it without my even noticing. "I'm so sorry. What do I owe you?"

"Don't be silly. This was most certainly my treat. Now I don't want to monopolize your time, as I know you must be a very busy traveler. But... is there any way in which you'd like to perhaps stroll around the town a bit? Like I said, I'm off work today and well, I don't want to be pushy like that other guy. But I just don't want to part ways with you yet. Of course, I'd completely understand if you'd rather..."

Although this display was so sweet, I couldn't bear to watch him suffer any longer. "Jack, I'd love to stroll around with you. What else am I doing with my day?"

"Excellent. Have you seen the Tate Britain Museum yet?"

"Let's go!"

Jack whistled over a taxi and it followed the Thames River just a little way until we got to the Tate.

As we walked around looking at British art from the 16th century, Jack took my hand in his as though we'd been holding hands our whole lives. I had always been so self-aware with affection and sexuality that when someone took my hand, I felt the heavy presence of it in mine as though it were an alien entity. It wasn't so much that I didn't like to hold hands. I just couldn't not think about it. But with Jack, his hand made mine feel whole, like a difficult puzzle that found its tiny, last piece. Warm and soft and right. Breathe, Beth.

At around 3:45, Jack suddenly had a worried look on his face.

"Are you okay? Do you feel sick?" I asked.

"I've just realized there's one more place you must go and we are losing light, I'm afraid. Can you run?"

"Sure, I can."

He guided me out of the museum back into the crisp, cloudy air, which had become colder by the hour while we'd been inside.

Excitedly, he said, "We need to get to a Tube station quickly."

And so we ran, holding hands in the super-charged wind, to the Pimlico Tube stop which we took to Waterloo. When we exited the station, he pointed "that way" and our run turned into a light skip.

"It's so cold!" I shivered.

Jack slowed down just enough to wrap his arms around my waist and give me a tight squeeze. "Do you want my sweater?"

"You'd freeze! You're not even wearing a coat."

"I'm used to the London cold. Here." He took off his argyle sweater revealing only a long-sleeved t-shirt. I could see his arms better now. For someone so tall and thin, they looked healthy and strong.

I took off my coat, added the sweater and put the coat back on. I was now wearing about 200 layers of clothes. "Please tell me if you need this back!"

"It's completely fine, love."

After more galloping and skipping, we arrived at Jack's surprise destination. "Voila! The London Eye!"

"Oh yeah, this is that wheel thing! I passed by this!"

"Yes, that wheel thing," he said sheepishly, with a cute hint of playful ribbing. "And we're just in time to take a ride to the top." He once again took my hand and led me into a small area where he could buy two tickets for the giant Ferris wheel. I saw on the brochure that instead of rickety, old seats like you might find at a small-town fair, this wheel had tons of glass pods that each fit two dozen or so people.

The man at the counter said, "You're in luck. We're about to close due to weather, so this will be our last lift of the day. And I suppose it's because it's so cold, but there are very few people queuing up. So you will get an entire pod to yourself!"

Jack seemed very pleased by this news. "Jolly good! That never happens."

Jolly good indeed. It occurred to me that days like this never happened to me. The kindness of strangers was something I often found myself yearning for in California, despite its seemingly sunny disposition. But Jack didn't feel like a stranger. This was the kindness of something else…the kindness of a gentleman.

We were directed into a waiting area and then, I guess because there weren't a lot of others in line, it seemed as though we were instantly shuffled into our own, private glass pod. There were others on the wheel, but they were scattered about. Frankly, although I knew they were there, I didn't take them into my memory. Jack was all I saw in that moment. Jack and the willowy fog of my own cold breath.

As our pod started to rise in the air, he pointed and said, "Look, there's Big Ben! Have you seen that yet?"

I smiled. "I have now. I'm seeing it now."

"Oh we have a clever one, don't we? I like it!"

As we continued to rise, I saw the beginning of a dark copper sunset over the winding Thames. I saw the outlines of castles and apartment complexes and pubs, all one and the same from this height and in this state of mind. There were parks and schools and burial grounds. Hills and heaths and cobblestone roads. I could feel the history of kings and Imperial Rule and beheadings and velvet gowns. I imagined what heartbreak felt like for lonely queens and princesses, and also for bartenders working at that very moment. To have your heart ripped in half by an Englishman…I didn't even want to imagine.

The wind picked up and our pod shook a bit. Whoa! Jack squeezed my hand and we both smiled. And then suddenly, snow! At first, flakes trickled in like an occasional shooting star. Was that? Wait! Yes it was! Then the rare shooting stars of snowflakes gave way and became a full-blown snow-shower.

"Wow! This is so beautiful," I whispered, turning my face to see what remained of the cloudy sunset catch his face.

"It's perfect." His eyes, now looking as green as Hyde Park, lingered on me for a moment. They then expressed a sentiment that read: "Please forgive me, but I can no longer not kiss you." If only there were just one word for that. I'll bet the French have it. But English speakers don't, so thankfully we can read eyes.

He leaned in so gently that our lips just grazed one another's. And then his bottom lip curled into mine and I breathed him in as my mouth opened. That was the tipping point in my life between having kissed Jack and not having kissed him. And we could never go back, not that I'd ever want to.

This didn't feel dangerous. This first kiss with him, his mouth on mine, felt like I'd found a home for my angst. The snow, his breath, the cold, the wind, his sweater — this was my place in time. I didn't know yet that this exact moment would embed itself into the folds of my gray matter. That this kiss had just dipped itself into my memory like a rum-soaked cherry. Delicious, intoxicating and so, so warm.

The kiss continued as we descended in our pod to the ground. The door opened and a man cleared his throat. "Excuse me, lovebirds. Sorry, we had to bring you down early. The wind and snow have become a bit too scary to have you up there."

Jack looked a little embarrassed. "Oh, terribly sorry."

I just smiled, and floated into the snowy dusk. I then remembered I was wearing his sweater. "You must be freezing! Please, take your sweater back."

"I'll tell you what. Have dinner with me and you can keep the sweater."

"How about this? I'll have dinner with you if you promise to take it back." I removed the sweater and piled my thousands of layers of clothes back on.

"You've twisted my arm. Deal. How do you feel about French food?"

"I don't have any feelings on it one way or another, but I'm game!"

"Excellent. I will make you a lover of it, even though the English have quite the history with the French." He said this with such an appealing laugh and sparkle in his eye that I had to smile. "Do you mind if we go early? I know it's just now 5:00."

I wasn't hungry in the least, but being with him at any time of the day sounded like a good idea. "I don't mind one bit. Let's go!"

He waved down a cab and told the driver, "To Kensington, please!"

"Right you are," the cabbie said cheerfully and we bounded through the snowy streets, past hundred-year-old buildings and grouchy-looking city-walkers trying not to slip on the wet, icy roads.

****

Even though we arrived at the French restaurant just after 5:00, the winter London sky had already darkened. There were cream-colored lights strung across the ceiling and yellow striped walls. Lots of gold decadence and curvy chairs. Very French, indeed.

Jack tilted his head and asked he waiter, "Might we get a table without a reservation?"

"Oui bien sûr. Vous êtes deux?

"Yes, please."

"S'il vous plaît, follow me." He led us to a corner table, draped in a gray tablecloth. We sat down in the low chairs and yet I still felt like I was high above the river.

"This restaurant smells wonderful, Jack."

"It does, doesn't it? I'd heard about this place and always wanted to try it, when the right occasion arose."

"I'm flattered!"

"Oh you know you're an occasion. Don't play coy with me. Okay, you can play coy, it's actually quite sexy."

I jokingly said, "Oh stop, you," while motioning with my hand to continue.

A young female waiter brought over a basket of warm, doughy bread, which cascaded out of the basket. "May I get you something to drink? Some wine for the lady?"

Jack and I made eye contact and I shrugged a "sure." He replied, "That would be lovely, thank you. How about a bottle?"

She nodded. "Very well sir."

He looked at me with concern. "I hope that's okay. I don't want to seem too forward. I'm not trying to get you tipsy or anything so please, no worries if you'd rather not get a bottle."

I wanted to tell him I'd been tipsy all day without even having had one drink. I wanted to tell him lots of things. But instead I simply said, "A bottle sounds perfect. Thank you."

For the next two hours, I'm not sure I've ever laughed so hard. My ribs felt like they might split in half in the most wonderful of ways. He got everything I said and he said everything I liked. It was as if someone studied the jokes I found funny, the color of eyes I found sexy, the shape of the arms that would make me weak, and then created a mold and made Jack exactly to measure. All I know for sure is that I laughed harder than should be even allowed during one meal.

At one point, I noticed there was a skylight above us.

I motioned upward. "I wish we could see the stars tonight."

"We'd have to go away from the city for that."

"Okay, can I tell you something dumb?"

He poured us each another glass of wine. "Always."

"When I was four or five, my sister told me that the whole sky was just one big, bright sun. And when it was nighttime, someone took a giant sky-sized piece of dark purple velvet and placed it across the sky. They poked holes in the velvet and what we think of as stars, is really just the sun shining through in little pieces." I hid my face. "I told you it was dumb!"

"That's lovely. Honestly truly lovely."

"Okay, now you tell me something crazy."

"Okay here's my thing. I'm scared of water."

I picked up the water glass sitting next to him. "Boo!"

"No, not that kind of water. Like lakes and oceans."

"Why?" I asked, laughing.

"Because of that stupid movie. Teeth?"

"There's a movie called Teeth?"

"About the sharks? Isn't it called Teeth?"

At this point, we were both laughing so hard, I could barely see. "Do you mean Jaws?"

"Oh yes, Jaws. Because of Jaws. Plus, I can't swim very well, so it would make it harder to get to you across the ocean."

"True. Plus you don't want that pesky shark Teeth to get you!"

We kept laughing and laughing and falling into each other. It wasn't water pulling us under but it might as well have been.

When we finally walked outside, it was snowing even harder than before. This was no longer a romantic, sexy snowfall. It was sideways and heavy and there were not as many taxis on the street.

"Where are you staying? I need to make sure you get back okay."

I wrestled with the ridiculous idea of not telling him which hotel I was staying in. There was a piece of me that worried about screwing it all up by taking it too far. These past 24 hours had been utter perfection. With my track record, I'd add a few more hours to the mix, and he'd see all the flaws under my skin.

But of course, I answered, "I'm staying at the Savoy."

"How lovely!" After a few cabs went by, he was finally able to flag one down and we hurried inside. "The Savoy Hotel on The Strand, please."

The cabbie nodded and warned, "I'm going to have to go very slowly, which may up your fare a bit. It's either a higher fare or we drive straight into an embankment."

Jack looked at me. "Let's let the lady choose. Higher fare, on me of course, or would you like to drive off the side of the road, perhaps into a river?"

I pretended to mull this over. "Hmm, both sound very romantic. But I think I'll go with the embankment crashing."

Everyone laughed and the driver picked up on my sarcasm. It was England, after all. "Very well," he said. "But honestly, we're going to go about eight miles an hour."

Jack held my hand tightly during the ride. It never felt forced or awkward. Just safe and warm.

As we finally pulled up to the Savoy, he said. "This has been the most lovely day. It has just been a pleasure."

"I feel the same way. I don't even know how to…I can't even begin to thank you for making this last day for me so utterly wonderful."

"I want to kiss you, but I know that would be tacky in front of our, sorry sir, our driver."

The cabbie turned his head slightly so that we could only see the side of his face. "I'd offer to get out, but it's negative three degrees so I'd prefer not." The snow began to fall even harder and the wind picked up. Swoosh, a gust of whiteness fell on the top of the car and it began to rock. "Sorry, folks. I can't drive in this. I'm going to have to wait it out in the lobby, so let's wrap this up." That was the most forceful I'd ever heard an Englishman sound. I considered Liam for a moment, but then remembered he was Irish.

Jack paid the driver and we all got out and skated our feet slowly to the lobby. There was a pause hanging in the air. I wondered if he was thinking of coming to stay and I wondered if I'd ask him to. I didn't exactly know what to say, but I was definitely thankful for the snowstorm.

"You have to be freezing. Let's go make some tea in the room. Does that sound good?"

His teeth were literally chattering. "If it wouldn't be too much bother, that sounds excellent."

As we walked to my room, he asked, "How did you settle on this fancy place? I've always wanted to stay here, but never did."

"I can't believe I didn't tell you about my sister's gift! She got me this whole trip as a birthday present."

He gasped slightly. "That is some incredible sibling you have. The best my brother has ever done is re-gifted an ice-cream maker I once gave to him and his wife. He'd forgotten I'd given it to him and the following Christmas, he wrapped it up and gave it right back to me with this twit look on his face like he was so proud of himself."

I laughed. My hand trembled as I keyed into the room and I hope he didn't notice. "Well, here we are!"

"It's beautiful! You're very neat. It smells like fresh lemons or something."

"No, I'm not neat; housekeeping is neat. Usually, I don't like anyone coming in but I forgot to hang the sign."

I noticed him looking around. In my worry over not revealing too much, I suddenly felt insecure that I'd told him too little. Was he looking for clues as to who I was? Did my inexpensive backpack and purple, lavender body cream give him anything to go on?

And then it suddenly occurred to me that my suitcase was open just enough to see what was on the surface. What was on top? A handful of brightly covered, "ribbed for her pleasure" condoms. Jesus, Riley.

I saw him see them, and then look away. At least I think he did. Then he glanced at the teapot, and then the closet door, and then, me. "I think you actually still have snowflakes in your hair."

I shook my hair like in a commercial and joked, "Are snowflakes sexy to you?"

"They are." He came closer to me. "I don't want to make things weird and if you want me to back off or go down to the lobby until the snow clears, I'd completely understand. There's nothing you can do to ruin this evening. But I must tell you, I'd really like to kiss you again. In fact, I can't believe it has been hours since our last one."

And then I reverted to typical Beth behavior (or TBB as Riley and I called it.) I stuttered, "I, yes, I would, kiss me, yes. But I need to tell you, the condoms. If you saw the condoms, they were a joke. I didn't really...I'm not some...you know, American floozy. Although it probably seems like it right now. I'll be quiet."

There was what seemed like a four-hour lull, (although it was probably only about four seconds), he said, "What condoms? What are you speaking of?"

I softly uttered, "Um, nothing." And then I did something that was very UN-TBB. I reached my hand behind his neck, feeling his perfect hairline as it stretched across his beautiful neck, I gently pulled him toward me and I kissed him. For a second, we both laughed at my spontaneous passion, but the nervous grinning gave way to a deep, body-melting kiss that felt powerful enough to ignite a bomb.

After disappearing into each other for what might have been minutes or years, I said, "Could you excuse me for just a minute?"

"Are you calling that Irish guy?"

I laughed. "Yes, I am. I hope you don't mind. It just feels like the right time to reach out to him."

I went into the restroom and turned on the faucet so he couldn't hear me pee or scramble around my toiletries bag for some freshening-up wipes, lotions, etc. I quickly slathered on some orange-blossom scented body cream on the insides of my thighs, my arms and just a dash on my pelvis. Freshened here and there as fast as possible and walked back into the room to find Jack making tea.

"I chose Ginger Jasmine for you. I hope that's alright." He handed me a warm, inviting cup, its aroma filling the room. "Shall we sit?"

We sat down with our tea on two yellow, tufted love seats that faced a gas fireplace. Through a window, we could see white snowflakes fall against a starry, black sky. If there had been a horse and carriage, this would have literally been the stuff of fairytales.

He continued, "Erm, what time is your flight tomorrow?"

"Sadly, it's at 8:00am. Which means I have to be at Heathrow by six."

"Perhaps I shouldn't say this, as I know I only met you last night. But I'm going to miss you. Is that crazy? It is, isn't it?"

"Not crazy at all. I'm going to miss you too. I really am."

Jack blew on his tea and took a small sip. He then set his mug on the table and stood up with an outstretched arm. I stood and took his hand. He tilted his head and smiled at me in such a charming way, I quite literally lost my breath. Gently, he pulled me toward him and kissed me once again. But this time, he breathed me in so intensely that I was sure he could hear my heart pounding. Both of his hands were now resting softly on my shoulders, but slid down so they were at elbow level. He pulled me even closer, so our bodies were touching completely.

My hands were around his fit waist, outside of his Oxford shirt, which hung down to the top of his jeans. He whispered my name, "Beth," and I could no longer stop myself from touching his skin. I slid my right hand under his shirt to feel his waist, and then slid the same hand across his stomach, which quivered from the touch. He cupped my face and kissed me even more passionately, and each inhale, exhale, tilt of the head during the kiss was more electric than the last.

Again, he said my name, "Beth" and I hummed like a tuning fork. He took one hand and caressed the side of my breast so softly that my thighs felt like they'd been lit on fire. My body tingled like the slow buzz you feel when you smoke a strong joint or do a whiskey shot. I felt as high as a kite, but without the drugs.

I wanted all of this, exactly this, but more. I gently guided our vertically entwined bodies to the bed, and we both fell on it, not releasing our grip on one another. We continued to fall into each other as though we'd known each other's mouths for eternity.

I removed his shirt, fully exploring every crevice of his chest and arms and ribs. He then removed my sweater and shirt (simultaneously) and we both laughed as the shirt/sweater combo got stuck above my arms. But once they were fully off, he softly kissed my neck, then my breasts, and stomach. Do I stop this? Should we leave it here?

He spoke about it first. "I am just as happy kissing your beautiful face and having you lie in my arms. If you want to stop, I completely understand. I don't, I mean, I'm okay with any scenario." He was doing his adorable eye flutter/stutter combo.

"If any part of me wants to stop, it hasn't spoken up. What I mean is my mind may come up with all kinds of reasons not to be here with you. But the rest of me, it's all yours."

"Not sure exactly what you've just said, but I shall take it all with a note of positivity." He then unbuttoned my jeans and removed them. That electric buzz was now shocking me at full velocity, like a cell phone plugged into the wrong outlet. Or the right one, actually. He began kissing the insides of my thighs, which were no doubt my sweet spots. He looked up at me and our eyes met in this vacuum we'd created — a space in time that was only ours. A point of singularity that was brimming, waiting to burst into everything we knew and will ever know. At least that's what it felt like.

He so softly touched the outside of my underwear and then seamlessly moved them to the side so he could better touch me with his tongue. I didn't care if this was unlike something I usually did. I didn't want to be the usual Beth. This was London Beth. And this was Jack.

He took me to a place that night I'd never been. I'd heard about "out of body" experiences on silly TV shows about the paranormal but this night, this was the opposite. I was as in my body as I could ever be and for once, I had no reservations about being there.

I remember telling him I was ready, fully. But what happened next was even more magnificent. He said softly, "Beth, I want you more than I can say. But there is something so special about you, I know there will be a next time and if we wait, if we somehow just wait, it will make it even more lovely."

Still warm and tingling from his tongue and his voice and his words, I simply pulled him up on top of me and we held each other, breathing together, our hearts beating just out of time. I was so happy in this moment. There was only this.

****

I never fell asleep. Part of it was because I was too afraid of missing my flight, but the main reason was I didn't want to be away from him. Even though I knew our bodies would lie next to one another, I wanted to be awake with him as much as I could. At 4:30am, I sat up and reluctantly untangled from him. "I should probably start getting ready. I need to leave for the airport in half an hour."

"I'm coming with you to Heathrow, obviously." He stretched his long arms.

"You don't have to, you know. I'd love it, but please don't feel obligated."

"I don't in the least. Of course I'm coming with you. If we leave early enough, we could stop and get a scone."

I looked out the window to see the snow was falling even harder against the dark sky. The sun was going to take another day off, that was for sure. "I wonder how hard it will be to get a cab?"

"We might have to take the Underground. Get to Paddington and then catch the Express from there. Will that work?"

"I hate early morning flights!"

He kissed me on the head. "We all do. Let's get going, love."

I finished packing my stuff while he showered. I wanted to join him but realized we were running out of time. I took a few toiletries from the exquisite bathroom so I could always smell this day, this week, this city. I yelled over the loud yet soothing rain shower. "Going to check out downstairs. Meet you there?"

He defogged the giant glass shower door with his hands. His body was shimmery and I actually noticed how tall he was for the first time. Seeing his hair slicked back with thyme-scented shampoo was like peering into a parallel life, or maybe even a future. Either way, I was glimpsing something so intimate. On the one hand this intimacy seemed to have come too soon and yet it somehow felt exactly as it was meant to be. "Are you sure you don't have time to take a shower with me?" I couldn't believe a man with such a posh accent was uttering such beautifully sexy words to me.

"Don't tempt me, Jack." I considered tearing my clothes off and jumping into the warm, steamy square with him. I wanted to see what it would feel like to touch him while he was wet. But my Typical Beth Behavior was back and I knew the logical thing to do was to check out and make it to the airport on time. "I'm so nervous the snowstorm will make everything take a long time. So I should probably check out."

He blew me a kiss through the glass and I gathered my stuff, went downstairs and checked out of the most beautiful place I'd ever been.

Chapter Six:
Friday

Once Jack joined me downstairs, the concierge tried calling for a cab. "It seems they're slow to arrive this morning. I'm afraid the taxi drivers don't wish to drive in this mess. May I offer you a map to the nearest Tube station?"

Jack politely declined. "It's alright, thank you. I know the city well." He grabbed my rolling suitcase and handed me his arm. "We've got a bit of walk to the station. Are you up for it?"

I was up for anything with him, even if that meant stumbling around on an icy white ground in the freezing cold.

I almost slipped twice, but Jack caught me as we slowly made our way to the Tube station, which was mostly bare and creepily so. Finally our subway took us to Paddington Station, which, at now 6:00am, was a becoming a madhouse. Jack bought two tickets for the Heathrow Express.

"You're actually coming with me to the airport?" I asked, stunned in the loveliest of ways.

"Of course. I'm going to spend every last moment with you, if that's all right." He paused. "I swear I have a life. I know it doesn't seem much like I do, but I have a job and friends and everything."

I laughed. "Sure you do."

Just then, a loud, menacing alarm went off in the station accompanied by flashing red and white lights. A voice came over the loudspeaker. "Attention train riders. Due to a suspicious package alleged to have been left in the station, we're asking that you calmly exit until we have this matter resolved.

Frightened, I turned to Jack. "What do we do?"

He remained stoic. "I'm afraid this has been happening a lot lately. I'm sure it's nothing, but we'll have to go outside."

"In the freezing cold? Are you kidding me?"

"Sadly, I'm not. It probably won't be for long."

We, along with all the other people, so English and polite, shuffled calmly out the exits onto the unbearably cold and windy street. People tried to huddle under awnings the best they could, but many were forced to stand in the blistering sideways snowstorm. The snow was coming down so hard that it was blowing into my eyes, my ears, my mouth.

And just like that, it began to fall even harder. A large mass of snow had gathered on top of the awning under which we stood. As a particularly hard gust of wind blew we heard a crack, then a pop! A man in the crowd yelled, "Everyone move! It's going to break!" Sure enough, the weight of the snow combined with that nasty wind was too much for this overhead canvas awning to hold and slowly it began to collapse. Everyone jumped out of the way into different directions and luckily no one was hit by the fall. We'd all moved so quickly, there was no time to coordinate, so I grabbed my suitcase and went left when Jack, it seems, went right. The air became dense with an unlikely combination of windblown snow and icy rain. I could not see an inch in front of me and had no idea what to do.

I heard a woman nearby yell, "The station is back open, everyone," and I could make out shadows of people working their way back in, so I followed them the best I could. All the while, I yelled out Jack's name: "Jack! Jack, where are you?!" but I could not hear his reply through the wind or the bustle of the crowd. Surely, he's back inside, I told myself.

Once back inside Paddington Station, I became frantic. I did not see him, and in all of my determination not to "do the cell phone thing," we'd not swapped contacts. I looked up and down every platform. I went to the ticket counter and even the restrooms, where I stood outside for at least five minutes. I went back to the platforms and searched again. Due to the suspicious package scare, there were now more people backed up to get on trains. It felt like everyone was walking quickly in all directions, all around me and it was all happening so fast, I couldn't even make out faces. "Jack!" I yelled again, hoping he'd somehow hear me through the mess.

Ding ding. I heard a ringing and quiet honking. I looked up to see the Heathrow Express as it made its way to the platform. I asked the man next to me how often it came and he said because of the backup, probably only every half hour or even 45 minutes. I knew if I wanted to make my flight I had to get on this train. Maybe Jack had somehow already got on. Or maybe he made an earlier train and is waiting at the entrance of Heathrow. Do I stay or do I go? The doors opened and a conductor yelled "All aboard the Heathrow Express!" I stepped through the automatic doors and sat down. As the doors eventually closed, my heart felt like was on fire, just a hot tangle of anxiety. The train left the station.

****

So much confusion set in as the Tube barreled toward Heathrow. I was exhausted from not having slept the night before and Jack's smell was still on every part of my body. I could taste him on my tongue. I felt sick. How could something so ridiculous as weather separate us, when just an hour earlier, I had been in his arms? I obsessively hoped he somehow made it to the airport and would be waiting for me there. He had to be. The universe wouldn't have me come this far in distance and emotion only to play such a filthy trick on me, would it?

When the train arrived, the doors opened to a small platform with escalators leading up to Terminal Five. The snow had let up a little, but the air was still made up of frozen crystals. I didn't care that I was cold or that I was lugging around a giant suitcase, I paced the platform back and forth and back and forth, at least 15 times. Just weaving in and out of rushed people whose cold breath you could see in the air. But there was no Jack. Maybe he'd gone up to the terminal? I took the escalator up and with each person I saw — each person who wasn't him — my heart sank a little more.

I couldn't call, text, even send him a cute little heart emoticon. Why had I picked this week to go retro and unplugged? I had figured we'd have time for all that info-exchange stuff when we were saying goodbye. I couldn't have possibly anticipated any of this! I looked up at the departures board to see that my flight was delayed. At first I was hopeful. I felt maybe that would give him enough time to show up. But after frantically searching every nook and cranny of the terminal and scanning the crowds for as long as I could, I had to get in the security line. As I took off my shoes and loaded my bag of toiletries into the bin, my eyes completely welled up with tears. I knew that once I went through that line, there would be no kiss goodbye from this perfectly lovely man who now was no longer a stranger.

Oh stop being so dramatic, Beth. You'll find each other on Facebook! This thought briefly comforted me as I put my hands up to be patted down for whatever it is they pat you down for these days. And then it hit me like a ton of radioactive bricks: We had never even told each other our last names.

In the 32 hours of knowing Jack, with no cell phone and no reason to believe we wouldn't have a moment to exchange our information, it just hadn't come up. A last name is usually the first thing I ask when I'm getting to know someone. I want to picture their ancestry and more importantly, how my name would sound with theirs. (I did this with every crush in high school and continue, even with waiters.) Is Jack a Windsor, tied in the most romantic, glittery of ways to the Royals? Is he a Smith? A Goldstein? An O'Donnell? Every possibility leads to tunnels of hypothetical fantasies and made-up histories.

But I didn't have that answer. And he didn't have mine. I bought a coffee and walked to my gate, still subconsciously surveying the crowd. I racked my brain for what I did know about him. He was a barrister, he'd said. He had a brother. Oh wait! His friend was in the Beatles cover band! I'd just find out his name and contact Jack through him. What were they called again? Lucy in the Sky? The Blackbirds? It wasn't coming to me and but I took a deep breath and told myself I'd figure it out later. I would find him, of course I would. Or he would find me. Surely, having the knowledge that someone named Beth lives some-where in California is enough to find her, right?

Tears started banging on the inside of my eyes again, and this time I let them fall. I figured I needed the release, even if I did look crazy to all of these reserved English folks. No stiff upper lip for me, that's for sure. I stuck my ear-buds in and waited for them to call my flight. All the while, I kept my eyes peeled for Jack because maybe, just maybe.

****

Once the plane began to lift from the runway, I looked out the window. I saw that what had once been a raging snowstorm had become mere stray, wet flakes, neither romantic nor phenomenal. Just indifferent and cold. I didn't want to watch an in-flight movie or play a video game on the console. I just wanted a gin and tonic and to sleep. It was too early for the former, so I put my coat against the window, put my ear buds in and closed my eyes. I hoped that when I woke up, I would be back at the Savoy, back in Jack's arms. Instead, I woke up to turbulence and snoring. A sweet old song came on and so I turned it up and tried to breathe hope into my confused and broken brain. I had a realization that nothing as incredible as love was going to come that easy to me. I was going to have to fight for it — to solve it like a mystery. And I was up for the challenge.

Chapter Seven:
Back To Life Before Life

Riley wanted to hear every last detail, at least twice. I obliged the best I could, but left out some of the more graphic details of Jack and my final hours in the hotel. And then I couldn't hold back anymore and told her those details too. Since I didn't have my phone while I was with him, I had no pictures. He'd taken two of us: one on the London Eye and the other the night we met, inside the nightclub. He'd shown them to me for "approval" and frankly, I remember not caring as much as usual. I was living in a dream where the angle of my nose didn't matter as much as the absolute abandon I was feeling. And none of it mattered now anyway because I would never see the pictures. They were taken on the event horizon of a black hole where they would remain frozen in time, never to escape the pull of the void and never to get sucked in either. They would sit still in that limbo, that land of oblivion and there was not a single thing I could do about it.

Riley did not approve of my negative attitude. "Okay, let's break this down. How many Jacks could there possibly be in London?"

I looked at her, as only one sister can look at another who has said the dumbest thing ever.

"Okay," she conceded. "Let's Google Beatles cover bands in London. Sure, there might be more than one, but we can find them. Right?"

I nodded with my head face down in the pillow.

"Ooh, here's one. The Revolvers. Is this them?"

"It's weird because I usually remember everything, especially everything that matters, but I cannot recall. That could be them?"

"Let's check out their site. Okay. They seem pretty old. Were these guys like in their 80s?"

"No. I don't think so!"

"Why don't we just try to find the contact info for every Ringo in every group? We'll reach out and one of them will be able to help."

I sat up, a light-bulb going off in my head and then immediately burning out in the worst way. "Wait, it just occurred to me that maybe Jack doesn't want to be found. Maybe he took off? Seriously, what else could explain this? Did he get picked up by a gust of snow that carried him to Kansas, like Dorothy?"

"Well technically it would have carried him to Oz."

"What?"

"I mean the weather didn't bring Dorothy to Kansas, it brought her away from Kansas."

"Riley, I love you for so many reasons. But please, don't focus on the least important part of the story. What I'm saying is, what if he decided the only way out was to leave me there?"

"So you're saying he bought himself a train ticket to the airport and then faked his own death?"

"That's exactly what I'm saying."

Riley continued typing furiously on her computer. "Okay, now I'm officially ignoring you and will later check you into an insane asylum. But first I'm sending a shit load of emails to fake Ringos across the United Kingdom. I'll start with this old guy." She began reading her composition out loud: "Dear Ringo guy from band. My sister…" It went on from there, this wacky story about how he might be our only key to unlocking this mystery of true love. I'm sure the fake Ringos will receive it well. Crazy Americans, they'll say. And they'll be right.

****

Over the next few weeks, I checked every old email account, Facebook and Instagram for any sign of Jack. Had he found me somehow? I spent most of my downtime at work Googling "Jack, London, Barrister, Soul-mate" and no clues appeared. A few of the Ringos wrote Riley back to say their bands had been defunct for ages, but that they hoped it would work out. One of them proposed marriage to her, as he turned out to be a guy from India looking for his green card. She respectfully declined, but mentioned that I was single.

As weeks turned into months, my confusion turned into anger, which turned into deep blues. To have something so lovely slip through my fingers just like that seemed worse than never having it at all. Had it really happened? Had I gone so insane that I completely fabricated an entire person in my mind?

I hadn't washed the shirt I'd worn under my many layers of clothing since I got back. It smelled of The Savoy's perfumed lavender soap and him — the undeniable scent that just was him. I'd take it out of the drawer and put it on for just a few hours, as if somehow its scent would give me the power to know where he was, or what had happened to him. I'd always put the shirt back into a deep corner of the drawer, however, never wearing it outside. I felt to do so would wash him away somehow. But slowly that scent was fading into the cheap cedar that housed it and as it drifted away, anxiety moved permanently into my stomach where it sat, eating away.

****

As this inner turmoil continued, I obviously continued living my life the best I could. I'd go to work, and when really pushed I'd go out with friends, many of whom patiently listened as I regaled them with every single detail of this ridiculous affair.

One night in particular, a few of my girlfriends and I were at a loud restaurant, when the hilarity of it all came over me like a spotlight. Drunkenly, I exclaimed, "So yeah. I meet a guy, finally a great guy, have this night, and then HE FAKES HIS OWN DEATH TO GET AWAY FROM ME." I raised my glass for a toast and my girlfriends joined in. "Hear, hear! To faking your own death."

My friend Jill laughed. "Beth's back, everyone! That funny friend who we thought we lost to London five months ago? She's back!"

Again, glasses were raised, cheers were made. My buddy Amanda added, "Plus, screw London. I bet he always had a scarf on, didn't he?"

"Yes, but it was very cold. He was right to have one!"

She continued mocking. "But I'll bet he's the kind of guy who would, like, always wear the scarf, even in 80-degree weather. Whatever, you need a big, strapping American guy."

"I don't need anything. I don't want to talk about Jack anymore. I'm fine, guys."

I was not fine. But it was time I started faking like I was. My life was not going to end at 30. Frankly, even I was sick of my story, so they had to be as well.

Chapter Eight:
Jack's Version

My name is Jack Stoll and I'm an Englishman born in Stratford-upon-Avon. My family moved to Hempstead Heath when I was a baby and I've lived there ever since. I have one brother, Stephen, who also happens to be my identical twin. We're relatively close, but in my family he is considered the over-achiever and sadly, in their eyes I'm the slacker. Most of this isn't due to work, as we're both barristers, although he has more prestige. No, it's because he's married with two children and I'm single at the age of 35.

Personally, I'm not bothered by this fact. I'm a bit of a perfectionist and by all accounts, I've only been in love once. Well one-and-a-half times, but we'll get to that. The first woman with whom I fell was called Natasha. She was a beautiful Ukrainian whom I met when traveling to Nice, France when I was 23. She was mysterious and temperamental and incredibly sexy. I didn't know exactly what love was supposed to feel like but I knew I couldn't extract her from my brain for years.

And though I wrestle with whether or not it was true love on my part, I do know she never loved me back because she told me so. Practically every day. But it didn't stop me from trying to pursue her for two-and-a-half years after we first made love. I finally gave up when she moved to Vienna and got married, which I suppose is a perfect time to give up on expecting reciprocity. And once I let her go, I did finally realize that we probably wouldn't have worked out. Mainly because I'm fairly certain she had ties to the Russian mob, but no need to dwell on the past.

From my mid-20s to now, many of my mates have tried to set me up with friends, cousins, one time even an aunt. I've had a few girlfriends, but nothing serious and nothing that lasted terribly long. Pleasant enough, but just never quite the right fit.

I spend an awful lot of time with work and family events and hobbies. I especially love playing cricket and my quiz trivia pub team, at which I excel. I suppose this all makes me very nerdy, but as a man in his mid-30s, I'm okay with that label. In fact, it's an honor to represent the nerds in my community.

When my mate from university called and asked if I wanted to go see his Beatles cover band that Wednesday, I initially declined. I had to get up early to work on a brief and also, well you know, it was a Beatles cover band.

"Jack," he said. "We never see you anymore. Honestly, when was the last time you came to an alumni function?"

I racked my mind and couldn't remember. "I know, but I'm an old man now. I can't get out and about like I used to. And doesn't it start at some ungodly hour?"

"You're 30-something, you don't have a walker. You're coming. I'll leave your name plus one on the list."

"Oh a plus one won't be necessary, mate. But okay. I'll try to make it."

"There is no try when it comes to the Beatles. It's really a jolly fun night. I know it's late, but we promise to make it worth it."

I hung up feeling stressed and bored. Bollocks, I guess I'd go. Although I'm pretty sure their silly band didn't count as an "alumni function" but alas. I spent the rest of that Sunday tidying up my flat and listening to the chilly November rain as it pattered on my window. I wondered if I was destined for a life of practicing law and being mostly alone.

****

When Wednesday rolled around, I'd frankly forgotten my plans. I put in a full day at the office and it wasn't till 8:30pm that my Google calendar alarm went off. I'd written it in as "Stupid Late Night Show" and I immediately discounted it. But then I decided I was hungry and okay, I'd go out for a quick snack and if I could get my energy up, I'd swing by the show.

I double looped my scarf (it was cold!) and I hopped on the Tube to find a restaurant near the club that didn't seem too crowded. After ingesting a warm, delicious shepherd's pie and a half pint of Harp, I sat for a moment feeling relatively content. Bored, but content. I checked my phone for messages (there was only one from my brother asking if I'd be in town for Boxing Day), paid my tab and walked back out into the frigid air. It was 10:00 and I'd made it this far into the night, I might as well show up and get it over with. If nothing else, this could count as my "alumni event" for the year.

As I rounded the corner to make my way toward the venue, I heard a man speaking loudly with an Irish accent. "Beth," he repeatedly said, his drunkenness as plain and as raw as a sunburn. Their less-than-charming banter continued for about 15 seconds and then I heard subtle yet unmistaken fear in her voice. Was that an American accent? This didn't matter at that moment, as it sounded as if a woman might be in trouble. I looked around to find them and then, across the street, I saw two figures in the shadows: a man standing awfully close to a woman seemingly without her consent. I walked over and saw he was holding onto her wrist.

"Excuse me, mate " I said. "The woman asked you to let her go."

The man turned his red-nosed attention toward me, his tone defensive. After a few jabs back and forth, he surprisingly backed down quickly and skulked off back to the bar with, I'm pretty sure, his middle finger held high. But wait — let's back up for a moment. Before I even dealt with him, before my initial "excuse me mate," I inhaled the most exhilarating whiff of her perfume. It smelled of honey and citrus and maybe bubblegum? It was so American that I almost felt guilty for enjoying it so much.

After the man's charming exit, I asked the woman if she was okay. And it was at that moment that I really took her in. Her hair with specks of red, her petite frame, her perfectly ski-sloped nose. But then she smiled. It was a weak smile, one which looked nervous and drained, presumably from her previous encounter. But it was a smile nonetheless. And for just a second, I couldn't catch my breath.

I asked if she was okay and she seemed embarrassed but genuinely grateful. "I don't know how I got myself into that mess," she confessed, and I did my best to convince her that HE was the wanker, not her.

We introduced ourselves, "Jack" and "Beth," and I immediately loved the way she said her name. Almost like she was saying, "Bath" like those 80s Valley Girls I used to hear so much about. She had just one dimple on her left cheek and it really stood out when her smile became more comfortable and alive. I wanted to crawl inside that dimple and make a home there.

Because my mind is so often 100 steps ahead of my mouth, I feel as though I stuttered for the next five minutes. "Would you…maybe…I realize I…erm, Beth, is it?" She suffered this for quite some time until the warmth of her eyes softened my tongue and I was able to spit out my request, which in retrospect was ridiculous. Yes, I invited her to the Beatles cover band show. All I knew was, despite the fact that I didn't know her from Eve, I didn't want to leave her side.

By some strange cosmic happening, she agreed. The American agreed to an adventure with me! For a moment, I questioned her sanity. Here, she'd just had this run-in with a strange guy and yet she trusted me enough to accompany me to a bar? I loved how non-cynical she was. I loved how spontaneous she was. And did I mention, I loved her unbelievably perfect dimple. I was so glad I'd decided to leave the house.

****

After our first glass of champagne, after I heard her laugh for the first time, after her arm gently brushed mine as we stood among the small crowd waiting for the band, the electricity in our space got sharper. At first, I was embarrassed that I'd dragged her to such a silly show, these nearly middle-aged men dressing in costume. But after I made a mocking remark, she leaned in with such sincerity and said she liked it.

At one point, "Paul" started singing "For No One" and I looked at Beth only to see tears in her eyes. My body softened in a way I hadn't felt before. I wanted so badly to wrap my arms around her. Not so much to "fix it," but to let her know how much I loved that she was moved by the song. And now adding to her laugh and her sense of fun and that dimple was the fact that she was a sensitive music lover. I wondered which lyrics she was specifically connecting with. I tried to watch her without seeming creepy, and I noticed she wiped her eye when he sang, "You stay home, she goes out. She says that long ago she knew someone. But now he's gone. She doesn't need him." Was it the lovely melody or was it something about those words?

When the show was over and I hired her a taxi, I knew I only had a few seconds to make my move but there was no way I was letting her leave without at least giving it a shot. She climbed into the back seat and rolled down the window. I stammered, even more than I had earlier in the night. I don't remember exactly what I said, but somehow enough words came out to get the point across that I wanted to see her again. She seemed to hesitate, but then agreed to meet me for lunch/tea the next day. There was that smile again! I must have told her the name of the restaurant at least 40 times, but she remained gracious and promised to meet me there.

I'm nearly sure I didn't sleep one minute that night. Would I see Beth again? Would she get cold feet? I could not remember ever feeling so strongly for someone I'd just met and I felt embarrassed by this crush I had on a virtual stranger. But that citrusy honey smell was all over my skin and she'd gotten herself right under it.

I may have dozed for a moment, but when morning came, I was up, showered and dressed in a flash. I called my boss. "I'm going to be working from home today. Feeling a bit of a cold going on." My boss seemed to buy this ruse and I didn't feel the least bit guilty for lying, which was quite unlike me.

Even though it was only 11:00am, I decided to cab it over to the tea shop so I could catch my breath and try to look as cool and casual as possible. I got there at 20 past and waited, waited, waited, my sweat glands threatening to explode at any second. I sipped water, read *The Guardian* and tried not to look at the time. As an American man might say, "Hey man, I'm just being Jack right now. Super cool, totally no big deal." I tried to channel that California-inspired cool guy voice in my head, but my uptight English nature overrode it and I continued to be nervous.

At just after noon, a stab of cold air hit my face as the front door opened. There she was. What was left of the sun hit the copper flecks in her hair in the most inspiring of ways as she walked toward me. That warm smile. Those crinkly, sweet eyes. She immediately apologized even though she was nearly right on time. The breath I'd worked so hard to control for the last 40 minutes had now escaped me again. I muttered something and hoped it made sense.

The rest of our time there was charming and easy, as though we were somehow old friends who'd been set up on a strangely successful blind date. Her lips were glossy like a rain-soaked rose and again, that smell of honey and fruit was so sweet that it overtook me. Maybe it was nothing more than just our pheromones co-mingling in the microscopic packets of light between us. Maybe she felt none of what I was feeling and I had gone mad. Maybe I'd never know. All I did know was that I simultaneously wanted to have her lips on mine and also hear her voice, letting every single word that came from her brain land in a safe spot.

Oh and she was funny! Mostly self-deprecating humor and bits about her mentally unbalanced family. Even when she got a bit dark, her eyes shone so brightly, it all seemed to even out. She said her job was boring and I recall attempting to respond by saying something like "anywhere you are couldn't be boring," but I think a bunch of nonsense spilled out instead. I couldn't read her completely, but I didn't think she minded.

She offered to split the check and I of course refused. I needed the extra time pretending to figure out what the tip should be in order to come up with the right words to convince her to spend the day with me. I didn't quite come up with those words, but somehow I got my point across. And as luck would have it, again she agreed!

I knew we didn't have much time, though I wanted to take her everywhere: to the park in Hempstead Heath, to the Scottish Moors, to Wales, to the moon, to my bed. But I instead settled on the British Tate Museum, as I thought it would be romantic to dive through history together. To pretend we had always been together from before time to the 16th century to now. We held hands as we walked around the gorgeous (and surprisingly empty) museum halls, taking in the art and each other.

Then I got suddenly struck with a genius idea! I needed to take Beth to the London Eye so she could see the beauty (albeit rainy beauty) of the city from a great height. Sure, maybe it was a little cheesy and certainly what some of the more established might call "new money" or worse, a tourist trap, but I didn't mind. Since I knew she had only a handful of hours left on the trip, I wanted to be able to say, "Here's everything in one fell swoop." I wanted to hand her the city in the palm of my hand, cradling her face with the other.

Time was of the essence, as we were losing light! I asked her if she trusted me and if she could run in her shoes. In what seemed to be typical of her disposition, she said "sure," seemingly without hesitation. I took her hand and we ran to the Tube station, carried by the iciness of the air. The light was running away from us and sprinting ahead, so we had to hustle.

When we got there and she realized what we were doing, she seemed excited. I bought our tickets and, because no one seemed to want to brave such cold, we had an entire pod to ourselves! Up, up, up, we went and as though we'd timed it with the universe or whatever controls the destiny of romance, it began to snow over the copper-toned city right on cue.

And then something came over me and I could no longer ignore the magnetic pull I felt toward her mouth. There is really no other way for me to describe it. Biochemically, and on a quantum level, there was no way the neurons in my brain could re-group or re-fire in a different direction. They were full-steam ahead toward a target with her face on it. Guns blazing. If electrons are supposed to repel, the atoms in every single one of my cells expelled all of mine, converted them into protons and attached themselves to hers. There was no bloody stopping it.

And so we kissed. Her full lips were soft and her tongue was warm and buttery as it enveloped mine. Snowflakes danced on the glass and then froze, in the same way our mouths — and time — seemed to. We were here, at this place in this time and it was so very lovely.

In the history of England and Europe with America, there was something called the Columbian Exchange, where many goods, animals and plant species were traded with the indigenous people. (Diseases too, but that's another conversation.) This was the time when America, certainly, and even much of Europe as we know them today came to be, because of this intermixing of people and things. For me, this mixing of Beth, this beautifully unique and foreign American and me, an Englishman who was open to an invasion, with our different mouths and viewpoints and accents felt like our own version of that. Would it ultimately bring destruction or success? I couldn't know. I just wanted to kiss her.

As luck wouldn't have it, the pod slowly started descending earlier than expected. The moment, the kiss, however, lingered in the air like a snapshot. And speaking of, this seemed like the perfect photo-op so I took a picture of the two of us. She faced me, laughing, her hair covering most of her face. I looked like a mental patient, but it didn't matter.

We were told that due to the snowstorm, they couldn't continue operating the machinery. We laughed like secondary school kids because the bloke seemed embarrassed to have caught us kissing.

Again, I had to think on my feet in order to keep the day/night going. She offered to give the sweater back I'd lent her earlier. "I'll tell you what. Have dinner with me and you can keep the sweater." She agreed to the dinner, but insisted on giving the sweater back, which was lovely and also appreciated, because I really was freezing although I would never have admitted it. I chose a French restaurant in Kensington and luckily we were able to find a taxi and a table without a reservation.

Everything was clean and had a golden hue. Warm lights, warm bread and the feeling that I didn't want to check my phone messages or Facebook or email. I just wanted to talk to this woman sitting in front of me. We drank and talked about everything and laughed about more. Not only was she beautiful and intelligent, she made my sides hurt in a way they hadn't in years.

When we finally left, it was bone chillingly cold and the snow was coming down hard. I didn't want to seem forward but I couldn't part from her in such a dramatic, icy fashion. I was worried about her getting back to her hotel safely so I (stuttering all the way though) asked if I could accompany her. She might have hesitated, but I was too cold to tell. I do know she said yes and revealed she was staying at the Savoy on the Strand.

In all my years in London, I'd never seen weather like this, so it was no wonder the taxi driver was nervous. I couldn't quite blame him, as the roads were bloody terrible. When we finally got there, (going a snail's pace), our cabdriver quit. Well, that's a bit of an exaggeration, but he did dramatically announce he was not going to drive anymore until the storm let up. We, the three of us, shuffled slowly on the icy driveway into the lobby, where the taxi driver sat down. This left Beth and me to have what could have been an awkward conversation.

I was about to say something stupid like, "Well, I can take a nap down here, good night," when Beth, bless her, said, "You must be freezing. Let's go make some tea in the room!" Yes.

I felt like I was floating as we walked to her hotel room. I was nervous and excited and completely content, somehow all at once. Whatever was going to happen there, whether it was us just talking or kissing or completely stripping off our clothes and ravaging each other, was going to be okay. The only issue weighing heavily on me was how little time we had left.

She keyed in and I gasped at how beautiful the room was, down to every last perfected detail. It smelled like Beth. So clean and American and fresh and hopeful. As I was taking in the surroundings, my eyes immediately were drawn to her suitcase, which was open on the ground. Sitting just on top of her poorly folded sweaters were a great many bright purple condoms. Look away, Jack. Those weren't meant for your eyes.

She seemed so beautifully nervous and I noticed some snow had made its home in a piece of her hair. I mentioned this and she blushed and said something flirty, although I had a hard time taking in her words. I just wanted to touch her. But I felt the strange compulsive need to tell her that if anything felt awkward or if she wanted me to leave, I'd go and I'd still think of her as glorious.

Then she said the craziest thing. She began stuttering, Jack style, about how if I saw the condoms, they were a joke-gift from her sister and that I should not think of her as promiscuous (although I'm fairly certain she used the word floozy.) I tried not to laugh at this word and instead did the kindest thing I knew how in the moment. I lied. "What condoms? What are you speaking of?"

She seemed relieved, which translated into passion because immediately after I said this, she grabbed the back of my neck and she kissed me. And this kiss lasted for months. She was so warm and her body, so giving. Her small hands traced the back of my neck in a way that was both sexually intense and sweetly tender. I could have lived in that moment forever.

Lost in it all, I was jolted out for a second when she stopped to excuse herself to the restroom. Cold, I decided to make us some tea and I waited for her as it steeped. After she came out and we both took a few sips, I couldn't continue the evening without touching her again. I stood up and in a very strange way opened my arms like I was some sort of flasher. I don't even remember making the decision to do that; my body simply led my mind.

Luckily she was on the same page and followed my lead. She walked toward me and I pulled her in and kissed her once again. And this time, I wasn't going to let her go. The kiss grew into more and our hands began to move as we fell into each other. Somehow, we wound up on the bed and the heat from our bodies choked me a little. But her sweet smell trapped inside the space between us made me want to swim in her.

I was so lost in the moment, I hadn't even noticed she removed my shirt until I felt less hot. Her hands touched me in the tenderest way and every part of my body reacted. I said something to her, I'm not sure what, and she responded with an "okay to proceed" type answer. So I took off her jeans and kissed every part of her that I could think of. When I got to her thighs, she made a noise that shattered me in the best way a man can get shattered. I took pause for a second before taking off her panties, which incidentally were a pale pink color with white lace trim. But they were so beautiful and fell so gracefully on her hips, I decided I wanted to keep them on. So I simply moved them to the side and after kissing her perfectly flat stomach, I placed my tongue between her thighs and drew her in. Frankly, I inhaled her.

After hearing her react, my body did everything it could to climb inside of her. But my mind — my mental, ridiculous mind — told it to slow down, that Beth was someone special who you wait for. I knew she was set to go back across the pond, and I wanted to long for her. I wanted us to have something to pine for. Sometimes, I'm truly an idiot. I told her this, or some version of it, and she smiled and held my head in her hands before asking me to climb back up to her face.

We kissed some more and held on to each other, as though for dear life. I might have fallen asleep for just a moment, but woke myself with my embarrassingly odd snoring. Could Beth truly love a snorer? It's not like she could just run away; this was her hotel room, after all. But luckily she didn't remove herself or kick me out, so I felt like everything was going to be okay.

That is until I looked at the clock to see we'd have to be heading out soon. I must have realized this mere minutes before she did, because at about 4:30am on the dot, she sat up and said it was time. We both exhaled and kissed and started putting the room back together so we could leave. And then I could start waiting for her to return.

I couldn't leave the Savoy without using that ridiculously excellent rain shower. So as Beth packed, I lathered up, in an exhausted but blissful daze. When Beth walked in, I begged her to join me in the warm wetness. I'm sure it wasn't actual begging but in my head, that's what it sounded like. She seemed to think about it for a moment, but ultimately in our game of rock, logic, passion, logic won out.

As I'd feared, the cabs weren't running at full speed (or at all) due to the snow. I explained to Beth we'd have to walk to the Tube. Without even the slightest complaint, she smiled and took my hand and I guarded it (and her) for dear life as we made our way to the station, and ultimately to Paddington. I bought our tickets for the airport train and every step of the way, she thanked me. How could she think for one second I wouldn't go with her to the airport? Was she not feeling the way I was? Because if she was, she'd never doubt that I wanted every single second with her to count.

Was I becoming soft? What was next? Was I going to buy a diary with flowers on it and start journaling? I laughed inwardly at the thought and then realized she was turning me into a romantic and I didn't even mind. And along those lines, the thinnest beam of light shot through the train station window, proving that the sun was desperate to meet Beth. It caught her hair and her cheekbone for a flash, illuminating her skin and the red flecks of her hair and then as quickly as it came in, it disappeared back into the snowstorm. But I caught it.

Just then, a loudspeaker announcement came on to proclaim that we had to leave the station due to the investigation of a suspicious package. Beth turned to me, worried, and I assured her this happened all the time. Although that was a bit of an exaggeration, it didn't really happen "all" the time, I had little doubt that we weren't actually in peril. I put my hand on the small of her back and we, along with quite an angry bunch, slid out of the station and into the cold.

The storm was now brutal. The flakes were flying every which way and it was becoming increasingly harder to see or hear what was happening around us. I held Beth as closely as I could, but as more and more angry travelers trickled out, they started bumping into us, making me lose my balance.

Beth looked at me. "What should we do? Should we leave?"

I told her it would probably not take too long and that we should try to stand under the overhead to avoid getting drenched. We inched over, clutching Beth's suitcase, and stood with a few others, shivering and nervous. I had wanted an excuse to continue holding her, but this wasn't exactly what I had in mind.

A loud, cracking sound pierced the air and piles of powdery snow collapsed on my shoulder. A muffled male voice yelled that the overhead was breaking. I reached my hand out to Beth to shield her and keep her safe, but my hand touched the air. I heard her inhale sharply and I suppose she must have moved in another direction because neither she nor her suitcase was still touching me.

The thick snow whirled so defiantly that I could barely see three inches in front of me. People were speaking in loud, panicked voices and it was hard to make out words. It was just sounds and cloudy air and confusion. Without my major senses, and in a panic, I moved quickly to the left. Or I was shoved, I'm not quite sure I remember. I came down oddly on the heel of my shoe and as I skidded on the ice I eventually lost the battle with the ground and fell so hard that the wind was knocked out of me. I couldn't move and for a moment I couldn't breathe, so I sat there, balled up, until I could find my speech again. Just when I was about to attempt to stand up, the last thing I remember is a man, in what seemed like a rush to get back inside, running toward me. And bam! His boot was on my face. I felt a pain like I'd never felt before and then, just blackness. And then nothing.

****

I awoke to find a man in a white coat shining a light in my eye. "Sir, can you hear me? Sir?"

I tried to speak but my throat was too dry so I blinked my eyes ferociously until he stopped holding them open.

The man called out, "He's awake!" Then back to me: "Sir, can you tell me your name?"

Again, I attempted to open my mouth, but confusion and a terribly severe pain prevented me. I cleared my throat and tried again. "Jack. I'm Jack."

"Jack, do you remember what happened to you?"

"No. Where am I? What's happening?"

"You were knocked down in the storm. You appear to have a concussion and some other bruising, so we're going to keep you here for observation. You're actually quite lucky it wasn't worse."

"Here? Where's here?"

"You're at St. Mary's Hospital. I'm Dr. Wallace. Can you tell me what year it is?"

As I shuffled through the card catalogue of my memories and thoughts to find the year, I paused for a second on a hazy detail that was trying to surface. "Wait, where is she?"

"Who is she, Jack? Can you tell us who?"

There had been a woman with me. A beautiful, soft, honey-like woman with hints of crimson and… a Californian? Yes, the American! Her name then surfaced as if it had been floating in my grey matter my whole life. "Beth! Where is Beth?!"

"We aren't sure, sir. But we will do our best to look into it."

I tried to sit up. "I have to find her. She must be here somewhere. Wait, what time is it?"

The doctor looked up at a clock on the other side of the room. "It's 2:00pm, sir. You've been out for over eight hours. Now, we need you to rest as we have to run a few more tests."

"Please, let me try to find her. I promise I'll come back. I'm fine. See? I'm sitting up! I'm fine."

A wave of nausea and dizziness came over me, which I tried to ignore the best I could. The doctor seemed to take notice as he motioned to the nurse to put something in my IV.

"Jack, I'm sorry. But we need to make sure there's no more swelling and certainly no internal bleeding before we can release you. We will do our best to find your friend, but as far we know, there was no one with you when you were brought in."

"Can I please at least call my brother?"

My cell phone, which they had laid by the bedside, was not charged, so the nurse handed me the bedside phone and told me how to get an outside line. I somehow remembered Stephen's phone number and left him a message. But what was Beth's number?

This didn't make sense. My memory was hazy but I know if I was hurt, she wouldn't leave me bleeding by the side of the road. Would she? No, she was lovely and kind and although I didn't know for sure, I could not imagine a world in which she'd do that. But then, what did I really know about her? Aside from the fact that her lips were soft, her scent exhilarating, her company thrilling and her laugh light and sweet? No, this didn't make sense at all.

I lay my head back down on the firm hospital pillow, and although my anxiety was ramped up, whatever was in that IV drip made me close my eyes and drift back into a sick, painful sleep.

****

When I woke back up five hours later, my brother was seated by my side. My lips were so dry they felt like they were cracking off and my throat hurt as much as my head. I must have groaned because Stephen stood up and bent over me.

"Jack, good, you're awake. I thought I was going to have to take your place on the throne and frankly, I'm not ready to be king."

"What are you talking about, you wanker?"

"I just wanted to make sure you knew you weren't really the king. You had quite a nasty fall, I've heard. Who bloody knows who you think you are?"

"Stephen? I need you to help me find the American."

"Oh dear, this was a nasty blow to the head. What American? What could you possibly be talking about?" He spoon-fed me some ice-chips.

"Delicious, thank you. That's right, I haven't told you about her yet. I met a woman, an American, Wednesday night and I know this sounds mental, but I'm pretty sure we fell in love. She was with me this morning and now I don't know how to find her."

"She didn't come with you to hospital?" He looked judgmental.

"Apparently not, but I'm sure there is some reason for it. There has to be."

"Well, what's her surname? I'll find her online."

"You see, that's the thing. We never exchanged surnames or emails or anything of the sort. She had this big thing about leaving her mobile in the hotel, so she could feel present with me. So all I know is her name is Beth. And she was staying at the Savoy Hotel."

"Well then you know her name is Beth and that she's very wealthy."

"No actually, it was a gift from her sister. This whole trip was."

"First we need to focus on making sure you're okay. Then, I'll just call the Savoy and get her info."

The doctor walked in carrying an X-Ray. "Good news. There appears to be no internal bleeding or swelling of the brain. You did suffer a slight concussion, however, so we will need to keep you here overnight. Your head is going to hurt for a bit, as is the wound over your eye."

I reached up and touched my eye. "Ouch! I was wondering why that hurt!"

"It appears that's where the boot came down on your face in the ice. You're quite lucky, this could have been much worse."

Stephen laughed. "Yes, Jack was always the lucky one."

The doctor ignored his sarcasm, but heaped on a little of his own. "The nurse will leave you with more instructions for the night. Hope you like Cream of Wheat for dinner!"

"Oh yes, it's my favorite cuisine." Everyone snickered supportively and a pain shot down my face. "Oh. Ow!"

The doctor noticed. "You're going to feel discomfort for quite some time. The nurse will give you some pretty strong pain meds that will keep you knocked out for the night."

I didn't love the sound of that because every moment I spent sleeping was one less minute looking for Beth. After I ate my gruel and was administered my pain med/sleeping pill combo, Stephen asked if he could leave for the night.

"How will you know the moment you become king if you leave?"

"I'll just feel it."

"Can you do me a favor? Can you please call the Savoy and track down Beth?"

"At your service, brother. And please, try not to slip on any more ice while I'm gone."

"I'll do my best, captain." I tried to salute him, but it hurt to raise my arm. So I half-smiled, closed my eyes and once again drifted off into a confused slumber.

****

When I woke again, it was Saturday. I jokingly asked a nurse if we were in the same year, and was assured we were. She didn't get the humor, however, and asked if I needed to speak with a physician. I told her I'd be quite all right and made a mental note not to make amnesia jokes when I was in hospital for a concussion.

My mobile rang and it was Stephen. "Hello? What is this thing? Who is this? Who am I?"

Stephen sighed. "Stop with the dramatics. I called The Savoy."

I sat up slowly. "Oh thank you! What did they say? What's Beth's last name?"

"Well, I've got a touch of bad news. They won't tell me her last name. Actually, they didn't even have anyone listed by the name Beth. But they said even if they did, they couldn't tell me."

This just wouldn't do. "Then we'll have to go down there and pay off who ever can tell us. Money is no object. I must know!"

"Actually, I went down there this morning because I really wanted to give you good news. I tried to pay the concierge, the doorman. No one would budge. I asked to speak to the manager, who said it would be a severe violation of their confidentiality agreement with guests. I pushed and pushed and finally he — his name was Dale — agreed to take a look at the list. He confirmed there was no one named Beth checked in this past week."

"That's impossible! Unless? Maybe she used her sister's name? I can't for the life of me remember what that was."

"How is it possible that you didn't get her surname?

"I have no real answer to that. I'm a complete buffoon. The nurse has just walked in, Stephen, I need to hang up. Thank you for trying."

"I'll keep at it. Let me know when I should come get you."

"Will do. Should be soon!" We hung up and I felt guilty for fibbing about the nurse. I just needed a second for this horribly frustrating news to wrap around me. I couldn't seem to exhale, which I'd hoped wasn't a side effect of this injury. I wasn't sure I'd ever be able to breathe out until I found her again. So I would keep gasping for air, with my bruised eye and headache and broken heart. Where was that flowered journal when I needed it?

After two days, I was finally allowed to leave the hospital. Stephen picked me up and I asked if he could take me to Paddington Station to see if perhaps Beth had left a note somewhere. He complained for a moment, something about being very busy at work. But after I used the "I almost died, Stephen!" line a few times, he finally complied.

He pulled over on the busy street and said, "You have ten minutes."

I jumped — well, as much as anyone could jump who was just leaving a hospital ward — out of the car and searched the station top to bottom. I asked train attendees, janitors, ticket agents, anyone I could find. I looked on the Lost and Found board, my heart racing like an actor who was looking to see if he'd gotten cast in a play. There was nothing. I went back outside and with the best forlorn look I could muster, asked Stephen if he'd take me to the tea shop we'd gone to. Less likely, but maybe?

Stephen reluctantly called his boss to tell him he'd be late and once again, he followed my romantically crazy orders. Again, no luck. I was plum out of ideas.

Last one. "I suppose you asked at the Savoy if there was a note left for me?"

"It was the first thing I asked Dale. He looked everywhere and said there was no note."

Having an identical twin brother is strange for so many reasons. Right now it felt odd because I could look at his face, nearly the same face as mine, and see perfect contentment. Knowing my face was battered and my eyes were so sad, it was so weird to stare at a version of me whose eyes were at peace. As if it gave me the chance to see what I'd look like if I only made better decisions — or had better luck.

"Jack, I think I should take you back to our place for a few days. I need to keep an eye on you. Would that be okay?"

"Of course. I love you, brother."

"Oh dear. Who have you become? Sentimental Jack? What, were you dropped on your head or something?"

We both laughed and I looked out the window at a warmed-up London as we headed to his family's home in Notting Hill.

****

You will never meet another man who checks his social media sites more than me, especially in the last two months since Beth disappeared. Every Facebook or Gmail notification brought a tiny ounce of hope that she'd somehow found me, but no such luck.

As a few more months went by, I reluctantly re-entered my life in the most normal way I knew how. I threw myself into work, never coming up for air. My boss seemed to take notice and rewarded me with a raise and some large high-profile cases. I wanted to keep myself so busy that I wouldn't even have time to think about what had gone so terribly wrong.

I spent many weekends with Stephen and his family and I knew I'd perhaps outstayed my welcome when his wife, Lydia, said, "Jack, I'm going to set you up with my old friend Fiona. She's lovely. And frankly, I think you need to find another way to spend your Saturdays instead of playing with my children. Don't get me wrong; they love their Uncle Jack. But sweetheart, I think it's time."

I personally thought this was rude and shot Stephen a glance, but he averted his eyes and stayed out of it. I assumed this was one of those tricks for keeping a happy wife: avoidance and denial.

After some nudging, I finally gave into Lydia's request and accepted the Fiona set-up. We emailed a few times and agreed we'd meet for an early dinner. Of course, the universe is a tricky mistress and she had to live just a few blocks from the Savoy. No one actually even lives over there on the Thames. But Fiona did.

I decided to be chivalrous and come to her side of town. My heart stuttered at every turn. There's the corner where Beth and I first met. There's the pub where we saw the cover band. There's the tea shop. Inside that hotel is the bed in which I tasted her. Jesus, I was really becoming disgustingly sentimental. Or just mental. Either way, it wasn't helping matters any.

Fiona and I decided on a curry restaurant about which I'd heard good things. I arrived first, as I so often do, and was seated in a corner table facing the door. I was looking at my phone when I saw a pair of long legs walk past the glass window and into the room. They were attached to an undeniably stunning, long-haired blonde woman. Her eyes were wide set and glowing green like a cat. She looked like a taller version of Kate Moss, and somehow even prettier. But she wasn't Beth.

"Hello!" She said, her voice raspier than expected. "You must be Jack."

"Yes, hi! Fiona, I take it?"

The conversation was already riveting. Don't judge so quickly, Jack. She seems lovely.

"That's me!" She leaned in and we kissed on each cheek. She sat down and the waiter immediately took notice of her and rushed over.

"What may I get you to drink?"

She thought about it for a second. "I'll have a whisky, neat. Top shelf, please." The waiter nodded, his tongue practically hanging from his mouth. She then looked at me. "Please don't be alarmed by my top shelf request. I do plan to pay my way tonight, so let me set your mind at ease straight away." She smiled and my anxiety softened just a bit.

"I wouldn't dream of that. I'm happy Lydia made the introduction."

"Me too. I can't believe she's been keeping this cute brother-in-law away from me all these years. I always thought Stephen was sexy and now I get to go out with his double!"

I knew she was making a joke, but I shuddered at the idea of being a double for my brother. "How do you know Lydia again?"

"We actually went to university together. She's lovely."

"Yes, she is." I couldn't think of anything interesting to say. Not one thing.

"She told me you had quite the strange story with an American girl."

"What? She actually told you about that?" I was immediately embarrassed and concerned about what I should and should not reveal.

"Well, I'd asked her for some interesting facts about you. She said you were a very smart lawyer. And I said, that's boring; I want real facts. What makes him human? She said your heart had just been broken by an American woman."

I sat there, stunned into silence. She continued, "I hope it's okay that I brought it up. What happened?"

Our waiter brought over her whisky. I'd forgotten to order so I asked him to please bring another for me. "We are certainly jumping right into this, aren't we?"

Fiona smiled. "We don't have to. Sorry. I'm nervous and when I get nervous I say the one thing I'm not supposed to say. And yes, I usually say it within just a few minutes of meeting someone." She softly put her hand on her head as if berating herself. "Stupid, Fiona."

"No, it's okay. The skipping the small talk thing is actually quite refreshing. No, no, I can talk about it."

She took a big sip of her whisky. "Okay, good. And then I'll tell you something quite personal and we'll be even."

My drink arrived and I, too, took a large sip. "There's really not much to tell. I met her on the street, actually not too far from where we are now. Some Irishman was yelling at her, so I stepped in."

"Yelling at her? That's awful!"

"He was some strange fellow she'd met and was trying to get rid of. So, I was basically her knight in shining armor and as you do with knights, you accompany them to their mate's Beatles cover-band show."

"Yes, that's one of the first rules of Knighthood. As ordained by the Queen."

"Yes, yes. So from there, we — how shall I put this without sounding like a complete and utter wanker — we proceeded to fall in love, or at least I proceeded to fall in love with her. We spent the next day and night together. Then somehow on the way to Heathrow, I lost her in a storm. And that's the story in a nutshell."

The waiter came back and asked if we were ready to order. Neither of us had looked at the menu, so I suggested to her that we have him bring out a few of their best dishes? She agreed, although stipulated that nothing be too spicy. "I don't understand," she continued. "You lost her in a storm?"

"It was that week of that terrible weather. Which doesn't really differentiate it from any other week in an English winter, but it was especially bad. No taxis were running that morning, so I was trying to help her — her name was Beth by the way — get to Paddington and then on to Heathrow. But at the station, there was a suspicious package alert and we all had to go outside in the storm."

"Oh how dramatic! How Dickensian!"

"Sadly, yes. As we stood shivering outside, an overhead fell and everyone scattered. I must have fallen on the ice and blacked out because the next thing I remember, I was in hospital. Beth wasn't with me and there was no note."

"But why wouldn't she have come with you? Did you call her?"

"I can't answer the first question but I have to believe there's a good reason. Your second question is more complicated. I never got her mobile number. Or her surname." I took the biggest swig of whisky I'd ever taken in my life. I felt a warm rush throughout my body and suddenly, it all sounded so absurd. Why was I telling her all this?

Fiona seemed to think it was absurd too. "But why? That doesn't make sense!"

"No, no it doesn't. But you know what? This was months ago now and I'd rather not talk about it anymore, if that's all right by you. Honestly, I can't believe Lydia even told you!" I wondered if, by asking about it, Fiona was putting me in the friend zone. I wouldn't blame her. I was a sad sack and not half as good looking as she was.

"Women tell each other everything." She laughed nervously. "I thought the most interesting part of the story was you blacking out and forgetting how you wound up in an emergency care unit! And yes, of course I understand. I've had strange things happen in my life too."

"Oh do tell! It's only fair." Our food arrived and after sniffing around the dishes, we scooped sloppy Indian food onto our plates. "Please, go on."

"I was once married to a Brazilian man. We met 12 years ago, back in my early 20s, when I was on a modeling shoot in Rio."

"This is already interesting."

"We only knew each other for four months before we got married, and were only married for two. We were back in London and one day, he just disappeared. Like completely vanished. I searched for him, and even hired a private detective to find him."

"Did you? Find him, I mean?"

"Yes, after a year, they found him. He had used me to get a work visa and had been living in Kent with another woman!"

"Bollocks! Did you talk to him?"

"Of course. I was able to get the marriage annulled and lots of paperwork had to be signed. He begged me not to, but back to Brazil he went, I suppose. I'm sure he married some other poor twit."

"I'm so sorry. I suppose if you're going to lie to someone and then cheat on them, it might as well be a beautiful model."

She chuckled. "Oh I feel so much better now."

"That's terrible and I really am sorry."

She picked up what was left of her whisky. "How about we make a toast? Just for tonight, we don't think about my idiot of an ex or the American? We just get drunk."

"I love this toast. Excellent." I raised my glass. "To Lydia for introducing us. And to whisky."

We clinked our glasses and finished off our first round. My gut felt warm, yet still a little empty. I decided to ignore the emptiness as best I could and forget the American ever happened.

Chapter Nine:
Beth Smiles

When you try to make sense of your life, a lot of people will say, "This is the way the Universe wants it to be. Don't question. Let go of the steering wheel," blah, blah, blah. I appreciate this point of view, but it always makes me wonder how true this could actually be. Does the Universe always get it right? For example, did the "Universe" really will my Uncle Albert to get super tipsy at Thanksgiving dinner and pass out, face first, in the pumpkin pie? It seems that's an odd plan for the Universe to make, so it's hard to take that philosophy super seriously.

In the seven months since I got back from England, I got a small promotion at work, joined a Tai Chi class and agreed, against every fiber in my being, to sign up on an online dating site. Riley set it up for me, using a slightly inappropriate picture from four years ago. In it, I'm dressed in a tank top and low-rise jeans with a fake sultry look on my face. I suppose guys who see it won't know I was being sarcastic, but I'm not so sure that's a good thing. When she asked what I should put in the "About Me" section of the profile, I said, "How 'bout something like, I repel men from all countries. They will literally flee from me. Good luck!"

Riley scrunched up her face. "Beth, take this seriously. You're not defined by one guy you met for a couple of days over half a year ago. C'mon!"

"I know. Fine. Write that I love dogs and TV."

"I'm gonna write that you love dogs and adventure. That sounds better."

"It sounds cheesy. But whatever you think."

She finished the profile and within six minutes, I already had four "likes," two "winks" and a message.

"What is all this? What do I do?"

We laughed as we scrolled through the early suitors. One guy claimed his name was "Adam Bomb" and he was wearing a crushed velvet purple suit in his profile picture. Another man, with the handle "Soy Latte" said his favorite pastime was to enter "break-dancing contests." And then there was the guy who sent a message. It read. "Dear London Lover." (I guess Riley thought she was being cute by picking that name.) "Your top is so fabulous. Did you get that at Express? Your lips are scrumptious. My name is Richard and I want to call you."

"Delete that!" I squealed. "Can he see that I read it? Delete!"

"Okay, so we haven't found the right guy just yet. Have a little patience. You don't need to write back to anyone. When the right message comes along, you'll know."

From the looks of the guys on these things, I'd need to have a lot of patience and that was most definitely not my biggest virtue. But Riley had been right before and so I figured I'd follow her lead. My instincts weren't exactly steering me in the right direction anyway.

****

Two more months went by and aside from the fact that I'd gained five pounds, I was feeling okay. Actually kind of back to my old self. It had been nine months since London and nothing had really changed. That is, until Riley called me at work with what she believed to be very exciting news.

"Guess what?"

"You won the lottery? Please tell me you won the lottery!"

"No, even better. I logged onto your account and…"

"Riley, what? You're not supposed to log into my account! That's private!"

"Oh what do you care, it says you haven't been on there for like six weeks. Plus at least I didn't sign you up for Tinder. That's way more intense."

"Ugh. No thank you."

"Well, you're lucky you have me because I was scrolling through your messages, of which you have many, and I came across one from a guy named Union Jack. Beth, that's gotta be him. It's your Jack!"

My heart skipped about five beats. Was it? Could it be? "Did you open it?"

"No, I thought you should do it. So go online, I'll stay on the phone."

After a small fiasco in trying to remember my password, I finally logged on, found the message and clicked on it. I could hear Riley's breath accelerating as the message loaded. "Okay, here's the message. 'Dear London Lover, if that's indeed your real name.' All right, that's kind of funny. 'I am really into England too, so much so that I chose this stupid name, which the site won't let me change for some reason. My name isn't really Union or Jack for that matter. It's Nick. I was on one of the swiping dating apps, but it made me feel dirty. So I gave in to this one. I still feel weird about it, but I think you're so cute and I'd love to know more. If nothing else, we could have some fish and chips somewhere sometime as friends? That's about the lamest thing I've ever written down. I'm going to stop talking...NOW.' Well, there you go. It's not MY Jack."

Riley encouraged, "Yes, that's true. But maybe this Nick guy is even better. Maybe THIS is the sign you've been looking for from the Universe."

"Will everyone stop with this Universe stuff? Enough already."

"Well, is he cute? Click on his profile!"

I clicked. And he was. Cute, that is. I tilted my head to the left to get a better view of his three posted photos. He had dark blonde hair and almond-shaped chocolate eyes. Were those dimples? Yes, I think they were. "Yeah, he is kinda cute."

"See? I knew this was a sign! Is his profile interesting? Is it funny?"

I started looking around. He'd written his "About Me" section, "Just a guy from Portland, who isn't as boring as I just made it sound. Is this thing on?" I read it out loud to her. He also wrote, "How about this? If by the time we're both 80, and we're not married, we go ahead and tie the knot. You don't have to let me know right away. Sleep on it. Man, I'm bad at writing these things." I read that to her too. "Yeah, he is kinda funny. Should I write him back?"

"Is that the dumbest question you've ever asked? Of course you should write him back? Let me dictate it to you!"

"No way! You'll have me proposing marriage to him by the third paragraph." I began typing, and reading it out loud to her as I went. "Hey Union. Is that a Danish name? It sounds Danish. Kidding, I know your name is Nick. Nice to meet you! Anyway, I'm new to this whole online thing too. It's awful, isn't it? Should we just take a European vacation together and see if it feels right? Is that how this stupid dating site works? I'll meet you at the airport in five hours. Go!"

"Beth, no, that's too much!"

"Obviously, I'm joking. If he thinks I'm being serious, then he's not the right guy for me." I read it over once and hit send. "Too late anyway, I sent it!"

"I'm so proud of you baby girl! Your first step to a better life!"

"Whoa, relax there Cupid. Let's not get ahead of ourselves."

"Oh shit, I gotta go. The baby's crying. I have a life too, you know."

"Bye sister sledge. Love you!"

We hung up and I stared at Nick's photos a little longer. I do what I'd assume many people do when they're "shopping" for dates on the Internet. I made up the story to go with what I thought I already knew having pieced together the tiny bits he presented. He looked like he's close to his mom. Maybe he grew up Catholic, alter boy and all, but gave it up after his first high school astronomy class? His mom wasn't happy about it, but she loves her son so they muddle through. From the picture of him near the ocean, it seems like he'd have a chocolate, no a yellow Labrador Retriever named Sam. He was in one three-year relationship, but that ended because she just wasn't funny enough. He works for an environmental protection non-profit and while it doesn't make him a whole lot of money, he feels fulfilled in his job.

As I continued spiraling down the rabbit-hole of fantasy, my in-box pinged. I opened it and whoa, it was a message from Union Jack AKA Nick! I wasn't sure if I could handle his on-line name. It was obviously a cruel reminder of everything from which I was trying to escape, but perhaps it was, ahem, the Universe's way of testing me. I opened the message. "Dear London Lover. I'm so glad I had my passport renewed last year so that I may take what sounds like a wonderful trip with you. I should tell you though, I snore. I feel like you need to know that before we go away together. Now that's settled, where at the airport shall we meet? Oh, and I look nothing like my photos. I'm actually a 14-year-old girl from Guam. Surprise!"

I literally laughed out loud. The old Beth would have called at least five friends, Riley included, to decode every word and construct the perfect reply. But the new Beth just didn't give a shit. So I replied back right away. "Dear Union, I've been waiting at the airport for six hours. I guess we got our wires crossed! Are we getting married or what? Do you think I should go ahead and sign us up for couples' counseling? You'll have to pay for it though, my insurance just ran out. Signed, Lover." I hit send and then turned my attention to the light September rain, which had begun tapping on my bedroom window. Rain was rare in this part of California and it was always welcome. I closed my eyes and thought of London Jack. I sighed, re-booted and thought of new possibilities.

****

I had a tough time focusing at work the next day. If I hadn't wanted distractions, I probably shouldn't have signed onto the dating site, because Nick and I sent messages back and forth the entire day. It turns out he taught high school English and although I was right about the dog (and oddly, the Catholic thing), he had a King Charles Spaniel, not a Labrador. Each message was funnier and more absurd than the last and I started daydreaming about what his voice sounded like.

I knew this much: I had learned my lesson about not falling too hard or too fast or really at all for someone I barely knew. It was nice to have this distraction, but I wasn't about to get sucked in. Granted, I was fast approaching the year mark since my visit to the UK, and I knew it was time to move on. But the tiniest little crystal, buried under layers of cynicism and doubt and logic, clung to the idea that Jack would find me.

That piece was so small that it didn't get a vote when Nick finally got around to asking me out. He wrote, "So I know I've built myself up to be quite the perfect guy on email. Would you dare to have your dreams dashed by meeting up in person? I would love to buy you a drink but I also don't want to destroy the fantasy that I'm super handsome. Best that I end this message now before I say something ridiculous."

I called Riley at work. "He asked me out. I'm going, right? He's funny! I wonder what he sounds like. We haven't even talked on the phone."

"Okay sir, yes. We will get that loan request processed right away."

"We're going to play a new game. It's called try to decode Riley's bullshit while she's at work."

"Very well, sir."

"So I should go? What do I write back?"

"This all depends. We will crunch the numbers and get back to you."

"You know I hate when people say 'crunching numbers.' Are you trying to upset me?"

Riley stifled a laugh. "No sir. I think you should get back to us with those documents and we will process them."

"You're saying I should write him back and accept?"

"Absolutely."

We hung up and I stared at the message a little longer. I had the strangest feeling of guilt and fear combined. What if I liked this guy and he disappeared into the ether? Would this keep happening to me? Jack was really only, oddly, the second time I opened my heart to someone, and both times they lit it on fire and then ran. Could I stand it again? I took a breath and hit the return button. "Dear Nick. When and where?" I hit send before I could re-think the matter.

Chapter Ten:
The Jack Dilemma

After our whisky-fueled night out, Fiona and I walked to the Tube station together. When we got to the entrance, she looked up at me, her breath laced with alcohol and her eyes pretty and mischievous, as if she were ready for a kiss or an invitation. I leaned in and kissed her. Although it was lovely, the spark I had felt with Beth was simply not there. It was just a man kissing a woman, without fire. I noticed she closed her eyes and when I pulled back again, she smiled. Maybe she felt the fire? Maybe I would never feel it again?

"This was really fun, Fiona. We should do it again sometime," I lied.

"I look forward to it. Thank you for a wonderful night out!" She gave me a quick but hard hug and then disappeared into the station, leaving only her flowery perfume behind.

When I finally got back to my flat, it was after midnight. I was perplexed by the idea that some people slip under our skin immediately and some don't. Why, when there are two women, both objectively attractive, both smart and seemingly kind and lots of fun to be around, would one make my guts do back-flips and the other, not? What is it about human chemistry or accents that control us? Or is it not about those things? Is it just a sense of calm or chaos, whichever we prefer, provided by another person, that gives us the rush or the relief we're looking for? Is it not about the other person at all? I was angry that love had struck me so hard and so fast and then literally knocked me out. And I was petrified that it wouldn't come round again and that I'd have to settle for less than everything.

****

My phone rang early the next day. The caller ID listed Stephen. Actually, that's not true. I have him in my phone as "Nitwit Brother," but regardless. "Hey royal spare," I answered.

"Hi Jack, it's Lydia."

"Oops, sorry, I thought you were my brother."

"Nope, it's me. I wanted to see how your date with Fiona went last night?"

"Oh yes. She was lovely. Quite lovely. Thank you for the introduction."

"I probably shouldn't tell you this, but I've already spoken to her this morning and she thought you were grand." She laughed and added sarcastically, "You understand, of course, I was deeply surprised by her reaction to you, but I thought you should know, she really enjoyed your date."

My first reaction was to feel flattered. "That's lovely, thank you for sharing!"

"You will be asking her out again, yes? When?"

I attempted my best American south accent. "Whoa, slow down there partner."

"What voice was that? You sounded touched."

"That was my John Wayne impression. I'm not sure when I'll be asking her out again, but hopefully soon. I just have so much on my plate at work."

I could hear her cover the phone and say to Stephen, "He might not ask her out again." Back on the mobile, she said, "Hold on. Your brother wishes to speak with you."

Stephen's voice sounded tired. "Hi wanker. You will ask her out again or it will cause a huge rift between my wife and me. Do you understand?"

"Oh when you put it that way."

"How are you, by the way?" He sounded genuinely concerned.

"Physically, I'm fine, thanks. Had a bit of a cold, but doing all right. Mentally, I'm a train wreck."

"I didn't want to try out my tough love training on you, but I think it might be time. Well, first I should ask, you're not feeling down because of that American, are you? This was almost a year ago!"

I lied. "No, it's just overall blueness. You know, just getting older and all that."

"You know one of the terrible curses of being your identical twin is I always know when you're fibbing."

"Then why did you bother asking?"

"Because, I need to say this. It's time to let go of all that. You met someone and had a nice time. That's it. We tried to find her, we couldn't; it's time to move on. We're still young, mate. You have your whole life ahead of you. Right? So come on. Buck up and all that. Ask Lydia's friend out again, please. If for no one else, do it for me."

"I'll try. I mean, I'll do it at some point. It was a nice night. I just wasn't quite smitten."

"What has become of you, brother? I think you could use a good roll in the hay, if you ask me."

"It's a good thing I didn't ask you, then. I've got a lot of work to do, so I must get going. But your request has been noted."

"In all seriousness, Lydia and I just want to see you happy."

"No, you want to see me miserable so that we can go on some sort of miserable double date. Cheers!" We both chuckled and hung up.

I made myself a cup of tea and threw myself into a Sunday of work. I supposed I would feel romantically inspired when I was good and ready. At least, I hoped I would.

Chapter Eleven:
The Nick Union

It took Nick a few hours to reply to my "When and where?" message. He wrote, "I suppose suggesting we meet at the grocery store right this minute isn't super sexy? So how about this Friday at Hoppers Pub downtown? Unless you've got a hangout you prefer? I am at your mercy! Man, that sounded lame. But I am!"

I thought about it for a minute. It was 6:00pm on a Thursday. I was home and having an especially good hair day. Why not allow the new adventurous Beth from London to continue? Maybe that was the lesson I was meant to learn there. So before analyzing it even further, I replied, "I liked your first idea. I live on the West Side. Can you meet at Gelson's grocery store on Lemon and Main? At 7? I think I'm semi-serious."

I realized how desperate this might sound after I hit send. But I liked the excitement and uncertainty of it. I hoped it didn't sound like I just wanted to "hook up" like on those sketchy apps, but I felt our previous emails implied otherwise. Before I could even get up to grab an iced tea from the fridge, my in-box pinged, yet again.

"I hope you're serious. I'll meet you there at 7 in the Deli Dept." Then he left his cell number.

Oh this thing was ON. It might not completely distract me from my insecurities, but it was intriguing nonetheless. I didn't have time to call Riley, as I had about half an hour to refresh my make up and get myself mentally pumped for whatever was about to happen. I did text her a quick, "I'm meeting Nick at Gelson's in an hour," just in case he turned out to be a serial killer or something.

Riley, not surprisingly, wrote back. "You're WHAAA?"

I ignored this and her three phone calls as I continued trying to hide the tired from my eyes.

My heart thumped as I got into the car and headed toward Gelson's. A flash appeared like a snippet of a movie: the memory of the same thumping heart when I went to meet Jack at that tea shop. This time it wasn't as strong, but I was just happy that my heart was beating at all.

I pulled into the mainly empty parking lot, parked, and sat still for a moment. Nothing to see here. I was just going to meet a stranger I met online in the deli department of a grocery store on a Thursday night, and all because I was having a good hair day. Breathe in, check for lipstick on the teeth, exit the car.

That heart-thumping thing was picking up, not necessarily based on my interest in Nick, but because what I was doing seemed so silly and strange, and also kind of awesome, hopefully. I walked straight to aisle 12 where the meat and cheeses were and there, behind the honey-backed ham, was a dark blonde wearing a Tupac t-shirt. He was facing away from me, so I approached with caution. I cleared my throat and he turned around and it turns out "he" was a "she" and she was Japanese.

"You're not Nick, are you?" I asked, and then immediately realized how ridiculous the question was.

"No," she said. "Sorry."

"Oh no worries." I was not the kind of person who said things like "No worries." But then, I wasn't really the kind of person who met strangers in the deli aisle.

Just then I heard a low, but soft voice behind me. "Beth?"

I turned around to see a man, with those almond-shaped eyes I recognized from the picture. He was taller than I expected, and wearing a green t-shirt that hugged his chest perfectly. "Oh? Nick?"

He smiled. "Did you think that woman was me?"

"What? No! Of course not."

"I saw you go up to her and you asked if she was me."

"You must be mistaken. I have no idea what you're talking about!"

The Japanese woman, who'd still been standing a few feet away, had finally been handed her deli order and as she walked off, said, "I hope you find that Nick guy."

He just looked at me and we both burst out laughing. This seemed like an awfully good start to this strange adventure. He extended his hand, "Should we try this again?"

"I think we're beyond handshakes at this point, no? Should we hug it out?"

"Yes!" He walked closer, his arms outstretched and bear-hugged me. His body felt warm and strong. "Much better!"

I laughed. "So how does this work? I've never had a first date at the grocery store before."

"Would you care to accompany me to the chips aisle, please?" He extended his arm, which I promptly took.

"Why yes, I would like that very much."

Arm in arm, we strolled over to aisle 6. He smelled like soap and licorice and his skin was softer than any man's has a right to be. He picked up a bag of salt and vinegar potato chips. "Do these strike your fancy?"

"They do!"

"Great. Now for date number two, let's go to the cookie aisle."

I started to feel weird that my arm was still linked to his as we gallivanted around. "Do you prefer chocolate covered cookies or say, sugar? Or ginger snaps?"

"They all sound delicious, but if I had to choose one, I'd go with chocolate."

He picked up dark chocolate Mint Milano cookies. "Your wish is my command. And lastly, please be my date for aisle 10." This time, it was the wine row. "Red, white, bubbly?"

"Oh I love a good glass of champagne. Doesn't even have to be all that good, for that matter. I just love the bubbles!"

"Got it!" He grabbed a medium-priced green bottle and then gently guided me to the check-out area, where he grabbed a bouquet of pale pink roses to add to the basket. "Now, if you wouldn't mind waiting by the exit. A gentleman never lets a lady see the bill."

"Is that an old saying? Okay, yes, sure." I awkwardly stood on the other side of the check-out section and fought the urge to stare at my phone. I looked at it once to see four texts from Riley making sure I was okay. I replied, "All good. Will report more later. XO" to which she somehow immediately replied, "You'd better!"

I watched Nick as he interacted with the checkout lady. His eyes were sweet and even though his hairline was receding a bit, he was incredibly handsome in a non-California type of way. He seemed outdoorsy without being rugged. Funny without being cartoon-ish. So far, I'd only walked a few aisles with him, but from what I could tell, there was an ease about him. At least I hoped there was.

As he pulled his wallet out to swipe his card, I felt a tap on my shoulder. "Beth? What are you doing?"

It was my friend Susan, who I owed a phone call to. "Hi!" We hugged. "So good to see you!"

"You didn't come to happy hour last week. Everything okay?"

"Yeah, just, was feeling a little under the weather. But all is good. How about you?"

"Everything is cool. Wait, why are you standing over here by the Coin Star machine?"

I wasn't much for lying and why should I? I leaned in close to her ear and whispered, "I'm on a first date. Don't look over. Don't say anything weird!"

She whispered back. "See? It's this kind of thing that makes me love you forever, even if you don't return my calls."

I motioned my head toward Nick to show her who he was. She looked at the exact moment that he walked over. He carried our bag of groceries in one hand and the flowers in the other. "Hi, I'm Nick. Are you our chaperone?"

Susan laughed way too hard. "No! I guess I could be! I wouldn't mind if you two are into that kind of thing."

I shot her one of those "please stop" looks that good girlfriends give each other when need-ed. She apologized with her eyes.

I stepped in, "Nick, this is my friend Susan. Susan, Nick."

Susan replied nervously, "Nice to meet you! Sorry, I've got to run, but you two, you know, um. Beth, call me soon!" She mimed a little phone in her hand and then took off, presum-ably before she'd even bought her groceries.

Nick watched her run. "Look at us, you're already introducing me to your friends!"

"Watch out! Pretty soon, I'll be demanding you meet my parents."

"I'm always game for that! So to begin. These flowers are for you." He handed me the beautiful bundle of pink roses, not so subtly conjuring up an English summer day.

"Why, thank you! They're gorgeous. Where ever did you get them?"

"Oh I have my own personal florist. He comes to my home and presents me with options."

"Well he did a great job!" I took a big whiff of the flowers and immediately sneezed.

"Yes, I asked him to put extra pollen in those, so I hope you appreciate that. Now for the second portion of our date. How comfortable would you be getting into my car?"

I hesitated for a moment. I thought the whole idea was that we were meeting somewhere public, no matter how odd, to keep the safety factor. But then I looked at the bag of chips, cookies and champagne and thought, what could this guy possibly do to me?

He noticed that I took pause. "You know what? I thought you might be freaked out by the idea, so I have a plan B. Would you care to take a little walk with me?"

"That actually sounds even creepier!"

"I promise, I'm only dangerous if there's a full moon. We're totally crescent mooning tonight."

New Beth, New Beth. "Let's do it!" It figured if I said those words, I couldn't back out of it.

"Okay, let's go! Come along!" We started walking down the side road that led up to the store. After about two blocks, we reached a gate that had a sign that read "Public Access until 10:00PM. Do Not Litter." Nick opened the gate and led us down yet another, somewhat steep path, which to my surprise ended at a park bench, overlooking a pond.

"Wait, there's a pond here?" I asked, excitedly. "I've lived here forever, I never knew that!"

Nick seemed cutely proud of himself. "Most people don't. Well, they might realize the pond exists, but not this cool little trail leading to it. Should we sit on the bench and partake of our dinner and Champagne?"

This was shaping up nicely. "That would be really nice. Yes!"

Nick removed the chips and cookies from the bag, opened them and laid them on one side of the bench. I continued clutching the roses while he began to peel off the Champagne wrapper. POP, there went the cork!

"Oh shit!" he said, which caught me off guard. "I forgot cups! Are you cool with just, um, swigging from the bottle? I'm so sorry!"

"This date is OVER!" I joked. "I mean, how DARE you?"

"Have a cookie. And please, have the first swig!"

"I'll start with the booze." He handed me the bottle and I held it with both hands. "Here goes nothing." I gently tilted it back and accidentally spilled a little in my hair and on my shirt.

Nick tried to wipe up my spill with the plastic grocery bag. "Not a party until a little bubbly gets spilled, right? Are you okay?"

Embarrassed, and with an immediate light buzz, I said, "I'm fine. I meant to do that!"

He laughed, handed me a cookie and took a swig of the Champagne himself. "Delicious!" He opened up the chips and we both grabbed a few, while staring out on the pond.

"So Nick…"

"So Beth? Tell me three things I should know about you that you haven't already told me!"

I considered launching into the tale about London and Jack, but then thought better of it. It was part of my story, I supposed, but I certainly didn't have to lead with it. In fact, I never had to share it again if I didn't want to. Plus, it wouldn't reflect kindly on me. Girl meets boy. Boy fakes being into it. Boy disappears? I knew I didn't know for sure what happened, but the truth was, it didn't look good. So instead, I answered, "Hm, let's see. I am a rocket scientist."

Nick swallowed the piece of cookie in his mouth. "Really?!"

"No," I said dryly.

"Well I don't know, you could have been!"

"You go first!" I took another chug from the bottle.

"Okay, I went to University of Oregon. I love football. And I think I really want to kiss you right now." Off my stunned silence, he added, "Too soon? Yeah, I know. It's too soon."

"You know what? This night is already strangely random and fun. Why not?"

"You're giving me the okay?" He asked again as he moved a little closer.

This couldn't have gotten more awkward. "Sure?"

He went for it, like someone jumping off the high dive. Scared approaching the edge of the board and then eyes closed, lean in and let it go, all at once. The kiss was sweet. He tasted fizzy and like a peach. His lips felt at ease on mine. I can't say I felt that "thing" I'd felt with Jack, but possibly that was a rarity I shouldn't expect again. It was nice. It wasn't rush home and write in my diary kind of spectacular, but still, nice.

He pulled back and looked at me for a moment. "Thank you. And now we've done that, so it won't be awkward the next time."

"Oh I have a feeling it will be." We both laughed. "Just kidding, yes."

We talked for two hours about our hometowns, our political leanings, current events. At one point, he held my hand and it felt really sweet. So much so that I leaned my head on his shoulder and left it there for at least three minutes! And for those 180 seconds, Jack didn't enter my mind one time. And it felt good.

Chapter Twelve:
The London Blues

After a month and much annoying persuasion from my brother and Lydia, I finally asked Fiona out again. On our third date, we went to hear an Americana band at a club in Covent Garden, and somewhere when the piano (and the tequila) kicked in, I started to get teary-eyed. Of course, this was unacceptable behavior from an Englishman, so I excused myself to the loo. There, I told myself to man up and get it together, which I'm not sure I ever did.

I liked Fiona. She was light and fun and easy to be around. She could hang like one of the lads, but smell pretty like a woman. And she didn't ask a whole lot of questions, which at this juncture, I really appreciated. I couldn't quite put my finger on why she wasn't making me feel more. Why the sight of her didn't make me want to throw up from nervousness or heartsick excitement, I didn't know. But for now, this was nice.

After another month and a few more dates went by, she wanted to have a "talk." We met up at a Turkish-owned café near my flat.

"So, Jack. Lovely, Jack." She started out saying. "We've been seeing each other a few months now."

I blew on my coffee and avoided eye contact as long as possible.

"Anyway," she continued. "I'm not looking for a label right now. But I did want to know, well, what your long-term game plan was. Like, do you want to get married some day? I'm not asking about me necessarily, I just mean in general. This is terrible, isn't it?"

"No, it's not terrible," I lied. "I'm not quite sure how to answer here. I do like you and I do enjoy our time together. I'm not sure what my ultimate plan will be, or if marriage is in my cards. I would love to make you a promise, but I simply cannot. I'm so busy at work and there's quite a bit of travelling I'd like to do. I am just trying to live in the 'now' as some guru might say. Is that…all right?"

She looked down for a moment. "I can't even imagine what I expected you to say. Of course, that's all right, it's only been a few months. I guess, I guess I just wanted to make sure that you didn't know for certain that I was not 'the one' as another person might say. If you know that now, please let me know." She seemed incredibly uncomfortable and rightfully so. "I can't, for the life of me, imagine why I didn't choose a pub with booze for this conversation." She laughed nervously.

I lied again. "I don't know for certain that you're not the one. Does that help set your mind at ease, even just a bit?"

She looked at me and smiled. "It does. I feel better, thank you."

But I didn't feel better. I felt awful and cruel and confused. But all I said was, "Good. Excellent."

****

It was Lydia who decided that Stephen and I should take a lad's trip. We decided on a small beach town in Spain. When I asked for time off from work, my direct supervisor (one of the firm's partners) told me that if I didn't go, he'd have me made redundant. He said I'd been annoying with my ass kissing lately and that he was tired of seeing me work so hard. It was making the others look lazy. This was all said with a wink of course.

Stephen made all the arrangements. He rented a villa for five days and even bought our flights, albeit on the dodgiest airline ever. "My gift to you," he said.

"I probably should be the one treating you. You've had to put up with my nonsense this past year."

"I like being the healthier twin. You know it gives me purpose."

When we arrived, I immediately felt better, I think mainly because I was finally out of London. There were no memories here yet, no landmarks that made me feel happy or sad.

They just existed for the sole purpose of my discovery.

Stephen began rummaging around the kitchen. "The person I rented this place from said it was stocked with booze. Ah, here we go! Right you are!" He found a bottle of decent vodka and some highball glasses. He proceeded to make us a couple of stiff drinks. "Now, let's go sit on the veranda and have a chat, shall we?"

"It all sounds rather ominous, but sure!" I accepted his cocktail and we slid out onto the balcony where we could see the Spanish sun was just setting.

"There's something I actually need to discuss with you, brother."

I groaned. "Oh dear Lord, please don't talk to me about Beth again. I promise you, I'm fine. I'm not insane, I've moved on. And things are progressing with…"

"No, you dolt. It's actually about me this time. Believe it or not, I have a life too!"

"Oh yes, sorry. Carry on."

"It appears that, well, it seems as though Lydia and I are going to separate for awhile."

My mouth literally fell agape. "You what? I didn't even realize there were issues there. When did this all happen?"

"We've been drifting apart the last year or so. Oh and I'm pretty sure she had an affair with one of her office mates. That hasn't been entirely confirmed, but nonetheless."

"Lydia? Really? This all seems so bizarre! This doesn't seem like her! Or you! And what about the kids?"

"We are going to share custody, 50/50. We're not entirely sure we will divorce, so no attorneys are present for now. This is just a trial separation. I've rented a flat near the Heath and decided to take this holiday until it's ready. We will tell the children together."

"Oh and here I thought this was true brotherly love that you wanted to spend time with me." Before he could react, I quickly added, "I'm just joking, of course. I'm so sorry about all of this. Is there anything I can do?"

"Yes, actually there is one thing. In order for our marriage to survive, you must marry Fiona. I know it's a lot to ask of you, but if you really want to help, this is the way."

I laughed. "Hardy Har Har. Okay, if that's the only way."

"No, there's nothing you can do except be here for me and Lydia and the kids."

I took a big sip of my drink. "I'll focus on just you and the kids, if that's alright."

"Now don't start saying mean things about Lydia just yet. We don't know what will happen and you won't want your foot in your mouth."

"I suppose. What I do want is a big drink in my mouth and this vodka isn't doing the trick. We need whisky and fast, yeah? Stephen, I'm really sorry."

"Let's not dwell on it just yet. Let's just have a nice few days away and hope it all gets sorted out."

I was never the biggest fan of Lydia but I knew she was an excellent mother to their children. It disheartened me to hear that a marriage, one that had mostly seemed too boring to be troubled, had cracked at the seams. It was these kinds of things that shaped my view of the whole traditional idea of matrimony and I was not only sad for my brother, I was sad that cynicism won the day.

We finally found some whisky and, after two more drinks each, we went to sleep in our respective rooms, all before 10:00pm. That night, I dreamt of turtle races and when I woke, I couldn't help but think the molasses-like slowness of my life was represented in my slumber. But today was a new day and I was on a beautiful Spanish beach. I would seize it, in the same way the Earth seizes the moon: by sheer gravitational force.

Chapter Thirteen:
Not All About Boys

It has been three months since our very successful grocery store picnic, and Nick and I are going pretty strong. He makes me laugh and he kisses me with sweetness. I really like the shape of his eyes and how they crinkle when he smiles, which is often. He's silly and romantic and I never have to worry about being too weird because he seems to like weirdness.

And yet there is something internal that feels empty, like a void that is simply not being filled. I am too young to be having a midlife crisis, although I'd always been filled with an inexplicable existential angst that I've come to embrace. I even try to convince myself that the part of me that is always searching is charming, even though I know it probably keeps me from feeling the highs that others do.

Riley suggested I see a therapist to try to figure it all out. I'm pretty sure that was code for "I don't want to talk about your problems so much, please go pay a professional" but I totally get it. I've been a weirdo for the past year (and really all the years that preceded it) so maybe she and my friends just needed a break.

I finally went to a counselor, on a Tuesday evening after work. I was immediately annoyed by the waterfall feature in the waiting room and the fact that Air Supply was playing on the radio. None of that soothed me, though I'm sure it was meant to. It just made me feel blue and like I needed to pee.

The therapist, Allison, called me into the small, cozy room, which smelled like sandalwood and vanilla. There were lit candles and a small, soft couch facing a chair. "Oh it's just like in the movies," I said awkwardly. "Like all that Freud stuff, right? Am I supposed to lie down on this thing?"

"You should do whatever feels comfortable, Beth, but most people just sit upright."

I felt like an idiot. "Okay, yes." I sat down and clutched one of the giant, fluffy pillows on my lap. "Very soft couch. Can I buy it? Wait, did that sound crazy?"

Allison chuckled. "I think I'll keep it for now. So, Beth. Tell me what brings you to me today."

We were getting right into this. "My sister thought this would be a good idea. To talk to someone about how," I searched for words. "I don't quite know how to express this, but basically how something just seems like it's missing from my life."

"Hmm. Let me start by asking, what is important to you in life?"

"I don't know. Family? Health? Love. Feeling like I matter."

"And how do you prove that you matter? What does that mean to you?"

"I find myself pining away for people, so enamored by what they do or who they are. It gets exhausting because I feel like I have nothing to give."

"Interesting. Gloria Steinem once said, and I quote, 'We are becoming the men we want to marry.' Does that make sense to you? What I think she means is why do we get so hung up on how great the guys in our life are, instead of focusing on how great we are?"

"I like that. It makes total sense! And it's exactly what I'm talking about. Like I have just kind of a boring job, and the same routine. I do the same songs every time at karaoke. I order the same thing from the menu of the same restaurants I go to. It's just, I don't know, boring."

"So what would un-boring Beth look like?"

Even though I promised I wouldn't, I then launched into the London story about Jack and the fancy hotel and my free-spirited attitude. How I'd felt more alive than ever before, not just because my heart had been revitalized but because I took chances. I let the wind (and English snow) carry me to places I'd never thought possible.

I heard myself tell her all this and immediately got embarrassed. "I know it's not like I jumped out of an airplane or anything. Or got on the back of someone's motorcycle and drove through the Scottish moors. I guess I'm acting like going for drinks or making out with someone I don't really know is a big deal. But for me, it kind of was."

Allison tilted her head. "What do you think changed in you in London?"

"I don't know; I let go of my schedule. I let go of my phone or the constant need for advice from my sister or anyone on what I should do. I just existed in the moment and it felt good. Oh and I could reinvent myself as whoever I wanted to be. He thought I was such a free spirit. So fun. He didn't see my stress or my fear. It was fun to be someone else!"

"It sounds like you freaked out a little when you couldn't find him. But maybe you actually found yourself instead? Maybe that's what the whole thing was about?"

I didn't have the heart to tell her that while I may have discovered a side of me I'd like to see more of, I actually really did fall in love in a day. Maybe that makes me crazy, but there was no need to share it with a shrink. The last person who needed to think I was insane was my therapist, right?

****

As I walked to my car from my session, I saw a billboard on a lamppost outside. It read, "Lead Singer Wanted for All Girls 80s Pop Band. Is it YOU?" I tore off one of the number tabs and stuck it in my pocket. Maybe it was me. Probably not, but maybe. I threw caution to the wind and texted Nick that we should take a trip to Vegas or L.A. or at least Reno. Somehow, within less than a minute, he texted back "When? Name it and I'll pack my bags!" I texted back a smiley face, went home and poured myself a glass of wine. Then I took out a journal a friend had given me for a birthday one year and I began to write.

I wrote until 1:30 in the morning. I wrote until my hands hurt. Actually, at about 11, I switched over to typing on my computer but the point is I wrote down my thoughts and feelings and before I knew it, I was writing everything I could ever remember feeling. I'm not sure what the point of it all was, but it felt soothing to get it out of my head and into the ones and zeros that comprise computer bits.

When I woke the next morning, I had a new lease on life. I wasn't sure if the therapist had anything to do with it, but it felt good nonetheless. I went to work and even my boss noticed I had a skip in my step. Something had magically awakened in me and for once, it didn't involve a man. Yes, it was fun seeing Nick, but he just enhanced the things I wanted to do. He wasn't the only thing I wanted to do.

The minute I got home, I called the phone number for the all-girl band. A woman with a deep voice answered. "Lacey speaking."

"Hi, my name is Beth. I saw you were looking for a lead singer for your band?"

"Yeah! We're actually holding some auditions this weekend! Are you familiar with like, mostly 80s pop and rock?"

"Yes! That's my jam!" I immediately regretted saying this. "I mean, I'd love to come audition. Where and when?"

Lacey gave me the address and told me to come around 3:00pm on Saturday. "We don't usually get rocking till mid afternoon. Everyone has day jobs, so we like to sleep in on the weekends."

"Perfect!"

"Have you ever been in a band before?"

I wasn't sure if I should lie at this juncture. But new and improved Beth was all about being comfortable in her own real skin. "I haven't, but it has always been a dream of mine."

"Great! Come prepared with an 80s song, preferably by a woman or girl band, that you can sing a cappella. Cool?"

"Totally. Thanks Lacey. See you Saturday!"

"Ciao," she said and hung up before I had a chance to reply.

I felt elated and out of my mind with nervousness. I had only two days to prepare. I found my fingers dialing Nick, which surprised me because this was usually Riley territory. I liked this.

He answered on the second ring. "Hi!"

"You will not believe what I just did. Wait, first, how are you?"

"I'm on pins and needles waiting to hear what you just did, that's how I am!"

"Well, you're talking to the next auditioner for a girl band."

Nick cleared his throat. "Come again?"

"That's right, I have an audition time on Saturday for this all-80s girl rock band or something. I don't know, I saw a flyer for it and figured what the hell?"

"This is greater news than when I found out robots could fly!"

I laughed. "That doesn't make sense, but I'll let it pass. What should I sing for the audition? I have to do it without music and it has to be an 80s song."

"What about something from Morris Day and the Time?"

"That's so random! But it gives me an idea. How 'bout 'Time After Time' by Cyndi Lauper?"

"Oooh, I like that! Sing a little right now!"

"I can't sing on the phone! But I have to go practice now. What am I doing? This is insane."

"It's not that insane. Someone must have told you to go live a little. That's what you're doing. You're living a little. Enjoy it!"

I liked the way he put this. "Yeah. That's right! And if it goes well, I was serious about the Vegas trip."

"Oh we're going, whether it goes well or not! But I promise you, it will go well!"

"Thank you, boo!" I had never called him a cute nickname before. I wasn't sure I should have until he warmly replied.

"Aww, boo boo. You get a double boo, that's how cute you are!"

"You're the sweetest. What are you doing?"

"I was just reading a book about the oil industry. Nothing all that exciting."

"Teach me everything you learn," I said jokingly. "Now I'm going to go live a little and learn the hell out of this song!"

"You'll be amazing."

We hung up and I signed on to YouTube to find an instrumental version of "Time After Time." I began to sing. "Lying in my bed, I hear the clock tick and think of you." And when I closed my eyes to think of Nick, Jack's face appeared. I wiped it out the best I could but it lingered like a spirit and never quite disappeared, even when I hit the final note.

Chapter Fourteen:
An Englishman In Spain

The dark, surprising news of Stephen's separation did not gel well with the cloudless, periwinkle Spanish sky. The serenity of our bungalow could only be described as other-worldly, especially since my "real" world was cold and rainy, lonely London. I put on my sunglasses, grabbed a towel and somehow persuaded my brother to head down to the beach so we could feel some much-needed warmth on our skin.

We rented a tiny sun umbrella and each ordered strawberry daiquiris, the girliest drinks we could think of. A few women walked by in tiny string bikinis, with the wettest, shiniest brown skin I'd ever seen. Then a few more ladies strolled past us, completely topless.

"Stephen, did you see that?"

"Of course. Did I forget to mention, this is a topless beach?"

"You did forget to mention that, yes. And while I find these beautiful lasses titillating, so to speak, I feel I'm at an outdoor strip club. Not sure it's really our style."

"Speak for yourself," he said half-heartedly as he stared at four more breasts walking by.

We clinked our giant, ridiculously shaped glasses. "You're really taking this Lydia thing hard."

In earnest, he replied, "I am actually. Let me just enjoy these days without feeling guilty or sad, if possible."

I suddenly felt horrible for being so glib. "Sorry, you're right. Carry on."

I pulled out a sci-fi book I'd been reading and shielded the topless beachgoers with prose about robots and flying saucers. Okay, yes occasionally I would take a peek, but mostly I was just happy to have a good book, warm sand, an eager-to-please sun and my slightly neurotic brother by my side.

I must have dozed for a few moments because I woke to Stephen punching me in the arm. "You're getting red, Jack and so am I. Let's go in and take a nap."

"Sure thing." This was truly my kind of vacation: being awoken from one nap only to go to a second location and take another. We grabbed what was left of our daiquiris and sunscreen, returned our rented umbrella and stumbled back to the villa. And it was there I had an epiphany.

"Stephen," I said, my voice weak from all the Vitamin D that had slid down my throat from the sky. "I don't think I'm done looking."

"None of us is done looking, that's why we're all so unhappy."

"No, I mean specifically, I'm not done looking for Beth."

"Lord, we're not going down this path again! You don't even know her. You've got a great job and family and Fiona to focus on. This is your early midlife crisis and I won't allow you to wallow in it."

"I don't think it is though. I could see how it still looks that way, but I can't get this particular girl out of my mind. And I don't think I've done all I can to find her."

"We've scoured the internet in every way possible. You don't know her surname or the name of her town or I'd suggest going there. It's one of those tests where you're supposed to learn to let go." He then muttered to himself, "I've got to stop reading these self-help books."

"It is a test, yes! It's testing my perseverance. The gauntlet has been thrown and I've not met the challenge."

"Jack, I don't know what you're talking about but I'm a wee bit drunk and exhausted and my head is starting to hurt. Can we nap again please?"

"Of course." I took my book and headed into the living room to lie down on the couch and give Stephen his much-needed alone time. But I didn't go to sleep. I ruminated over every glance, every kiss, every curve and crevice of her body. I didn't care how long it had been or how long I'd known her. I was meant to find this woman and I was going to.

I Googled "American private detectives" and was overwhelmed by the amount of search results. I clicked on the first one, "Christopher McKinney, Private Eye" (who promised a free consultation) and bookmarked his page. I would call when less rum was streaming through my blood and I would soon prove to everyone that my heart had been right this whole time. I finally drifted off into another nap while thinking of Beth's freckles and the smell of her fresh, American skin.

Chapter Fifteen:
Time After Time

My hands were literally shaking when I opened the car door and headed toward the studio space where my audition was. Nick had wanted to come with me, but I of course immediately shut that down. I didn't need a witness to what could be the most embarrassing moment of my life. I did, however, tell him the address, just in case the whole thing turned out to be some sort of nefarious ruse.

I opened the unusually heavy door to find four women lounging on various chairs or amps. "Hi," I said, my voice very small. "I'm Beth. I'm here for the audition?"

A larger woman with dyed hot pink hair stood up. "Oh yeah, I'm Lacey. We talked on the phone!"

We shook hands. "Yes, hi!"

"I play drums. This is Alyssa, she's our bass guitarist. This is Becca, she's our lead guitarist. And that's Lizzie, she plays everything else, like the xylophone, washboard, whatever we need."

Lizzie waved. "We're called the Girls Of Summer, by the way."

Lacey gave her a semi-glare. "Name is still in flux."

I smiled and waved hi to everyone. "But you don't have a lead singer? How come?"

Alyssa piped up. "It's kind of a long story but she quit."

Becca chimed in. "She so didn't quit. We fired her ass. She was getting a little too flirty with some of our boyfriends."

Back to Lacey. "Not just our boyfriends. My girlfriend too."

I shook my head. "That's no good! What happened to girl code?"

Lacey nodded. "Exactly. So what are you gonna sing for us today?"

"I thought I'd do a little Cyndi Lauper? Is that cool?"

All four girls smiled in varying degrees. Lacey answered, "That's totally cool. Okay, we'll sit over here and you show us what you got." They moved their chairs and amps into one row and guided me to the front of the room. My heart was beating so hard, I began hoping it would act as a metronome. But it was skipping all over the place, as was my breath and my sweat. I was a huge mess. Why had I decided to do this?

"Okay. Here goes nothing. Sorry in advance." I laughed nervously and inhaled deeply. Shit, I was really doing this. I began too high. "Lying in my bed, I hear the clock tick and think of you." I cleared my throat. "Wait, can I start over?"

Sweetly, Alyssa answered. "Of course. Just relax. Breathe. We don't bite. We actually want you to do well."

I shook my hands off like I was drying my nails and exhaled. "Right, yes. Sorry! Okay." I started again, this time on key. And I closed my eyes and sang every word from the heart. "When you're lost and you look, then you will find me. Time after time. If you fall, I will catch you, I will be waiting. Time after time." I surprised myself with the number of tears that burst through the threshold of my performance, but at some point I realized it was par for the course. I'm not sure if I ever even once opened my eyes, which I guess is weird.

When it was over, I looked straight ahead of me, as to try to not make eye contact with a single soul. I felt shaky and liberated and elated and terrified. Lacey spoke first. "Beth, the only note I'd give you, personally, is to be a bit louder."

Funny, that's exactly what I was trying to do with my life in general. "Louder. Yes."

Lacey looked around at the other band mates. They seemed to nod and smile to each other. "Other than that, you've got the gig."

"Wait, what? Me? You want me to sing for you guys?"

Lacey smiled at my shock. "We could pretend to mull it over and all that, but you're the best we've heard and we really want to get back to the music."

"Just curious. How many women tried out for this?"

Alyssa answered. "Oh about 15. Or maybe 20."

"Really? And I was the best one?"

Lacey laughed again. "By far. To be fair, one of the women was in her late 70s, which is all good and all, but, seriously, you were perfect. You should know this about yourself! You've got some great pipes on you."

I couldn't believe it. "Wow, thank you so much. So what happens next?"

Lacey pulled out a piece of paper from a notebook she had next to her and handed it to me. "Our next gig is at the Ale House downtown three weeks from today. Rehearsal starts Monday evening at 7, here. Can you dig it?"

"I can totally dig it! Thank you all so much!" My heart was racing yet again. I felt so alive and so different in my skin. I hadn't even remembered the frontal lobe of my brain making the decision to do any of this, and yet here I was, standing before strangers, singing from my gut.

As I walked back toward the car, the oddest instinct came over me. I took my phone out, and didn't call Riley or Nick. Instead, I took a selfie in front of the building which housed my new band, posted it on Instagram, and hashtagged, "#TheNewMe." In my heart of hearts, I hoped that somehow, in some parallel universe, Jack would log on, find me and be intrigued. I knew the thought was insane and tragic, but I couldn't deny how I felt. And yet there wasn't a single thing I could do about it.

I went home and continued writing until my fingers hurt.

Nick called at 6:30. "You picked up! I can't believe you haven't called me yet!"

I couldn't either. "Just got in," I lied. "You're now talking to the lead singer of The Girls of Summer. Can you believe it?"

Nick screeched, "You got it! Really? Beth, that's so awesome! We need to celebrate."

Somehow my triumph had me a bit melancholy. I felt like an imposter, posing as a wanna-be rock-star, or a writer, or Nick's girlfriend. Everything was so good and yet the missing piece was all I could focus on. Had it really been Jack that made me feel whole those two days? Or was it London? Or something else entirely? These thoughts passed through my mind like television re-runs and thankfully, the credits finally rolled.

Deep breath, get it together Beth. "Yes, we really should! Wanna come pick me up?"

"I'll be right there! Sit tight!"

Chapter Sixteen:
Jack And The Private Eye

Mr. McKinney's office was small and smelled like leather. From a private detective, I expected frosted windows on the front door and clouds of cheap cigarette smoke, but he actually had a fairly large number of plants and New Age type crystals scattered about the tiny space. We shook hands when I entered the room and he motioned toward a tan armchair in which I sat.

"What can I do you for, Mr ..." he shuffled through his appointment book, "Stoll. Mr. Stoll."

"I am trying to find an American."

"I'll bet that's a sentence that gets uttered often."

I laughed. "Yes, you're quite right. So about a year ago..." I told him everything. Well, not everything! I left out the graphic details of our night at the Savoy and our first kiss on the London Eye. But I told him what I knew. Her name was Beth and she lived somewhere in California. I was able to backtrack and tell him the approximate date of her flight from the States to Heathrow. Surely, that would be enough, I figured!

"It's not much to go on, I'll be honest. Airlines are very stingy with the list of names of people on their flights. I'm not quite sure how I'd arrange that." He seemed nervous.

"Oh. Isn't that just, kind of, what you do? Figure out how to find these things? Slip the authorities a few quid?"

"Right, you'd think so. In the movies or on the telly, that's certainly how they'd do it." He seemed to slip into a state of utter panic at this point. He then began chewing on the backend of a pencil.

"Are you all right?" I asked with real concern.

"Quite fine, yes. Yes. Beth."

Just then my phone pinged. I looked to see it was a text from Fiona. "Where are you, handsome?" she wrote. I hadn't quite called it off with her, but our dates were becoming fewer and further between. Fiona was so lovely, but she just didn't make my mind race. I knew it was mental, but I had to face it.

Mr. McKinney continued muttering Beth's name.

I stood up. "This has been a good consultation, sir. But I must run." I honestly didn't think we'd get any further and I wanted to cut my losses.

"Very well sir. I am on the task. If I find anything, I will contact you and we will discuss the small fee. Otherwise, cheerio!"

"Excellent. Thanks again, mate." We shook hands once more and feeling defeated, I left his office. Granted, this particular idea had most likely failed, but I wasn't going to give up now. And who knows? Maybe he was some kind of crazy genius?

I stepped out and called Fiona. I asked her to meet me at a coffee shop we liked after work. I could hear in her voice that she knew what was coming. It was quite unpleasant for everyone, but had to be done. Even though it was absolutely bonkers, I wanted to focus all of my energy on finding Beth.

When we got to the coffee shop, she beat me to the punch. "I feel like I know what you're going to say, Jack, so let me make it easy on you."

"Fiona, I…"

"Just answer this one thing. Is this because of that girl? That American who left you to bleed in the road?"

I hated lying. "No. It's just that I'm no good for anyone right now. I've been in a funk and I just have to get myself out of it. I really do hope we can stay friends. I know that's cliché, but I find you to be so lovely."

She softened a bit. "It's fine, Jack. I wish you the best of luck. And yes, perhaps someday we will be friends. I think I'm going to leave now. I assume you'll get my tea."

"Of course, yes. Thank you Fiona for being so understanding."

And with that, her beautiful, tall legs directed her to the big, glass door and off she went. I sat for a moment, wondering if I was simply making every possible wrong turn. I guess time would tell.

Chapter Seventeen:
Nick Meets Riley

Somehow, in the four months since I've been seeing Nick, I've kept him at arm's length from most of my friends. Yes, he joined on the occasional pub night, but Riley had been really busy with work and their paths had yet to cross. She decided that would come to an end when she called to say she was having a dinner party that upcoming weekend and that if I didn't bring him, I'd be disowned as her sister.

Nick was immediately game and asked if he should make a dish. When I told Riley this, she actually squealed with delight. I'd never heard her make that noise before and it both pleased and frightened me. She assured, "I'll take care of the cooking. You tell him to just bring his charming self. And maybe some wine."

We were her last guests to arrive and we shared the table with Riley and Mark, Mark's co-worker Jason and his wife Theresa and an old childhood friend of all of ours, Cynthia, and her girlfriend, Lila. There were three open bottles of wine and a delicious homemade guacamole dish (with chips) in the middle of the table. The smell of sweet potatoes and rosemary chicken and garlic wafted in from the kitchen and everything was almost right with the world.

"So Nick," began Mark. "How did you two meet again?" Riley shot him a "look," but this didn't deter Mark one bit. "It was online, right?"

Nick glanced at me as if to get permission. I shrugged. "We actually met in prison, if you must know. She was a very tough guard. I was there because I'd tried to shoplift some Junior Mints. Big mistake."

Everyone laughed except Lila. "Is that true?" she asked.

We all laughed some more and never answered her question.

After dinner, while we snacked on chocolates and sipped cognac, Riley suggested a game of Pictionary. We paired off into two groups and Nick was as hilarious and charming as always. We, of course, won. I think mainly because I was able to guess his depiction of *Citizen Kane,* which was no easy feat.

We'd had to park a few blocks away and because I was wearing heels, Nick offered to get the car and bring it around. As soon as he left, Riley pulled me aside and told me she thought he was "the one." Off my contrarian look, she yelled, "Beth! Don't be an idiot. This guy is perfect!"

"I'm not saying he isn't. It's just too soon to know if he's the one. Sometimes it feels like something is missing."

"What could possibly be missing? He's cute, funny, smart and he adores you! And he didn't leave you stranded at a Tube station!"

"There's no need to bring that up. I wasn't even thinking about him!"

"Yeah, sure you weren't." She gave me a quick hug. "Be happy. That's all I want for you. But for what it's worth, I think this guy is pretty special."

The truth was I did too. But I couldn't shake that empty feeling that would occasionally crawl into the pit of my stomach so I decided to change the subject. "Oh hey! Our band is playing at O'Malley's next weekend. I'm so nervous. Wanna come and laugh at me?"

"Are you kidding? I wouldn't miss it for the world! Now go, he's probably outside waiting."

"Love you, you big galoot!"

"Love you too, you monster!"

Nick was patiently waiting when I got outside. I got in and kissed him passionately. No matter the hole in my heart, I was going to try to see if he could fill it. He continued to come so close that it was starting to seem like it might be enough.

****

By the time the next week rolled around, I was petrified. I couldn't eat for the whole day before our band's set at O'Malley's. I told Nick not to come, although I was okay with Riley and Mark being there. I wanted some support but just in case I failed, which was a strong possibility, I didn't need everyone witnessing it. I considered asking Lacey if she would ban everyone from taking cell phone footage, but realized that would sound crazy.

On Saturday, I couldn't breathe at all. I would try to take big gasps of air, only to take in too little and choke on my own oxygen. Maybe this being a rock-star thing wasn't for me. Lacey told us all to wear our most 80s clothing. I found an old, hot pink fluorescent bow in a Halloween costumes box, along with some bangles, rubber Madonna bracelets, a mesh top and leg warmers.

When I got to the venue, Riley and Mark were already there for some reason. "Jeez guys, they're not even open yet!"

Riley smiled. "We were just so worried we'd be late. We'll just go grab a coffee somewhere nearby. Do you want anything?"

"A barf bag, maybe?"

"You're gonna be so great. And you look hot! Look at you, Madonna!"

Lacey saw us in the doorway and waved me in. "Okay, go, go. I have to prepare. And by that, I mean I have to drink some tequila." I walked inside and followed Lacey to a greenroom, where the other women were tooling around on their instruments. Lacey announced, "Doors opening in 15 minutes and our set is in 45. They're not letting us do a sound check, so whatever tuning or warm-up you need to do, now is the time. And we each get one drink ticket, so use it wisely."

We scuffled over to the bar, grabbed some drinks and sat down. I put my head between my legs. Lizzie looked concerned. "Beth, are you okay?"

I didn't want to let on how terrified I was. "Yeah, just mediating." I took a giant swig of my tequila.

Lizzie laughed. "Oh the old Buddhist tequila meditation. Isn't that the one the Beatles did?"

A few of the women chuckled. And while they chatted and joked around, I sat in a quiet panic for the next half hour.

We had to walk through the crowd to get to the stage as the green room was behind the bar. The room was dark, but I could tell there were surprisingly a lot of people crammed in — at least 60. I could smell Riley's perfume as we passed down the aisle and onto the stage. The other women set up their instruments, did some quick tuning and Lacey approached the microphone.

"Hi O'Malley's! I'm Lacey and this here is the Girls of Summer, also known as the Andrew Ridgeleys! We haven't quite yet decided. I hope you enjoy our little flashback to the 1980s. We think it's a fun place to be." She backed up to her drum set and motioned for me to take center stage.

I felt like I should say something but when I opened my mouth, the only syllable that emerged was "Ah." I suppose sensing my fear, Lacey clicked her drum sticks four times and the band began to play, like they were part of a robotic animatronic Disneyland set piece. Right on time, my mouth opened and the words came out perfectly. I was in tune and holy shit, I was good! WE were good! Song after song, fast or slow, the crowd whistled and sang along. I hadn't felt that alive in…well, since London! It was invigorating and for that hour on stage, I didn't think about any boys, not even those across the pond. I thought about the lyrics and my cute 80s skirt and how much of an impact we had on the crowd.

And finally, it felt like whatever was left of the old Beth — her fear, her uncertainty, her angst — was gone. And I didn't miss her one bit.

Chapter Eighteen:
Jack's Determination

Much to the chagrin of Stephen, my depression inspired me to grow a raggedy beard. It was unlike anything I'd ever planned on doing, but I just couldn't be bothered to shave. The odd thing about it was more women hit on me than ever before. Something about that "I don't need anyone" look seems to make ladies swoon!

After I called things off with Fiona, I decided to take a break from dating, no matter how many women slipped me their numbers at pubs. I continued focusing on work and tried to act as the rock I knew my brother needed.

It had been three more months, and he and Lydia were still separated. He'd moved into my flat for a bit, but just last week he hired himself a month-to-month studio flat, which was all very depressing. I decided to give him a ring. "Hey, want to meet up for a pint?"

His voice sounded small. "Sure."

He hadn't moved far from me, so we picked a place nearby. I guess my facial hair had gotten even more out of control since he'd last seen me, because he audibly gasped. "What is that on your face? Why are you allowing this?"

"I actually think I look kind of dapper, yeah? Like a San Francisco college professor or…"

"Or a hobo? I mean, honestly!"

"Just trying something new out. How are you feeling?"

"Oh good days, bad days. It's really quite maddening the whole thing. But the kids seem to be taking it relatively well. How about you? Any new prospects?"

"Yes, actually. I have two appointments lined up with detectives next week. I am not going to give up."

"That's not quite what I meant. Jack, Jack, Jack. When does this end? Enough, honestly. This has become, dare I say, obsessive."

"I've been thinking a lot about it and I've decided I'm going to give it one more month. If I can't find her after this, I will stop. I assure you. But I won't be able to date or really do anything until I know I've given it a proper try. Okay? Can you give me one more month?"

"I suppose it's your life, isn't it? I just don't want to see you throw it away."

We drank a couple of more pints and we continued to reassure each other that we'd be okay. We were both good-looking, somewhat successful lads. As more beer seeped in and as we had more laughs, I actually started to believe I would be okay after all, with or without my stupid beard.

Like clockwork, a woman at the end of the bar sauntered over and began to flirt with me. She was very toasted and Stephen seemed appalled.

I joked, "Beard twin is off the market. But beardless twin…?"

Stephen quickly chimed in, "…also off the market. Sorry."

I turned to him. "So I guess you're not dating while you're separated?"

"Of course not! I have absolutely no interest in dating anyone right now. We don't yet know what we're doing."

"Of course, sorry. We'll be celibate together, how's that?"

"It's ridiculous on your end, but I suppose it's fine." We clinked glasses one more time and settled into our shallow alcohol haze.

****

The second detective I met with was a woman called Carol Willow, which frankly sounded made up. She took a 25-pound consultation fee, which she made clear was non-refundable. She listened empathetically to my story, but what seemed like hopefulness appeared to turn into despair when she found out how little I knew about Beth.

"I'm sorry," she said sincerely. "If the hotel refused to give her surname and the airlines won't comply, there's not much I can do. Maybe your best bet would be to go to California and just search for her yourself?"

That was a waste of 25 quid, although a tiny bit of me thought a soul-mate-searching trip to California might be fun. When I told Stephen Carol's suggestion, he asked politely that I not relay any more of this nonsense to him. He claimed he already had enough stress on his plate, he could not suffer my foolishness. I refused to comply.

The third detective was a German man named Gero. (He would not give a last name.) He actually wore a real fedora and smoked a cigar in his office! He did not offer me one. Again, I told him the story and he seemed perplexed.

He took a puff. "I don't usually comment on the emotional details of a case, but what was so special about this woman? There are so many and you don't even know her. And also Americans are so…so simple."

"With all due respect, she was anything but simple. Or maybe she was so simple, I found it lovely. Not simple in a daft way, but simple in her perfection."

Gero let out a groan. "I wish I hadn't said anything. Okay, let me mull this case over and see what I can do. I will call you within the week. Good day."

I suppose his abrupt salutation was his way of telling me to leave his office. Even though he wasn't especially effusive, I figured if anyone would get the job done, it was a cold, logical German man. I rode the Tube home, with a latte and a smidge of hope. I even considered shaving my beard, but then thought better of it.

Chapter Nineteen:
Nick Steps It Up

At the six-month mark of our courtship, Nick called and asked if he could take me out for a fancy dinner. I was in a bit of a funk, although his offer sounded lovely. Plus, things were going well at work, the band had quite a few more great gigs under our belt and since that night when I discovered that dusty old journal, I'd really gotten into the habit of writing. I'd even started writing some sort of a children's book about love. I wasn't sure where it would go, but it felt so good to be creative.

He picked me up at 7:00 and took me to a very sweet Italian restaurant downtown. He seemed oddly nervous.

"Are you okay?" I asked as I broke off a piece of bread.

"I am! Are you?" He was clearly sweating.

"Yeah. I'm good!" I wasn't sure what to say, but figured maybe he was coming down with a cold.

We both ordered cocktails and when they arrived, he made a toast. "To an amazing time with an amazing woman."

"Aw!" We clinked glasses.

"So I have to tell you something, but I don't want you to get freaked out."

Whenever anyone tells me not to freak out, I immediately freak out. I could feel my skin getting very hot and oily. My breath got shallow. "Okay? You're scaring me."

"No, I don't mean to do that." He took a big sip of his Moscow Mule. "I'm going to say something because I want to say it, but please, I don't want you to say anything back, okay?"

Now my throat was actually closing shut. "Okay?" I said mistakenly as a question.

"I know it hasn't been all that long, but Beth. I, well, I love you."

My lungs swelled with air. I had waited so long to hear these words again and yet when they penetrated my ears, I felt anxious and unsettled. But I also felt flattered and excited and like he truly meant it. He said it with such conviction and there was nothing about him that could possibly make those words sound cheesy or unwanted. And yet …

"Nick, that is so sweet. I … thank you."

"I hope I didn't make it weird, but they say when you know you love someone, you just know. And I know and wanted to share it with you."

We both smiled and continued to sip our drinks. "Thank you. I guess I'm not quite ready to … I'm not quite sure …"

"Like I said, please don't even think about saying it back. Unless you must!"

Our food came as I awkwardly kept my eyes on the table. It felt as if our waiter lingered for hours, even though it was only seconds. I thought it best to change the subject. "This looks incredible. This is so much fun! Thank you already for such a fun night!"

And then he burst. "And I'm thinking maybe we should think about moving in together."

The ice I'd just swallowed seemed to choose that moment to begin pin-balling down my throat. "You, what?"

"Just a thought. Shit, I wasn't even going to say that tonight. It's too much, too soon. But we spend so much time together anyway and my lease is up and it's not totally unheard of, is it?"

"This is a lot. But no, I'm glad you said it all. It's okay. I love spending time with you and you've given me a lot to think about. I've never lived with anyone, besides my parents and my college roommates. So, it's kind of a big thing. Have you? Have you lived with anyone?"

"My ex-girlfriend. We lived together for two years."

Oddly, this had never come up. "Oh, was this the most recent ex? Laura?"

"Yes, it was Laura. Sorry, I just didn't go into the details of it. But we lived together back in Portland."

"It's okay that you have a past, Nick. I'm not threatened by it."

"I didn't think you would be. It just never came up. But yes, I lived with someone. Anyway, just putting it out there. Let's enjoy our dinner and sleep on it and I promise it won't be weird no matter what happens, cool?"

"Cool!"

Our night, as usual, went on to be light and easy. Somehow I'd never told him about London or Jack and because I felt the need to be closer to him, I relayed it in all its absurdity. "I know, it's the craziest story, isn't it?"

"It only makes me like you more, if I'm being honest. I love that you have stories. I love that you took a chance. I hope you'll take a chance on me too." He paused. "Did that sound too much like an Abba song?"

"No, it sounded sweet." I raised my glass. "To online dating and deli meat."

"Now that is a toast that has never been done before. To original toasts!"

I laughed. "Original toast should be name of our band!" We continued laughing and eating and drinking throughout the night. Although a large question hung over us, it didn't darken the mood. I was confused though. Confused and a little bit excited. This caused me to perhaps drink a bit too much, but the night ended well and the morning hangover wasn't too excruciating.

****

After Nick left and I'd had my morning coffee, I of course had to call Riley. If a guy asks me to move in with him and Riley doesn't hear about it, did it really happen?

She answered on the first ring. "Yo, what up?"

"What is this, 1992? Who talks like that?"

"I'm tired. I'm doing laundry so I can't talk long."

"Oh you're gonna take back those words. So last night, Nick tells me he loves me and wants to move in together."

Riley immediately yelled to Mark. "Honey, you're on laundry duty now. I'll be on this call for awhile!" Back to me, she screamed, "He WHAT? That's awesome, right? What did you say?"

"I said thank you!"

"Beth!"

"I don't know if I love him yet! It's way too soon. Isn't it? I don't know how I feel!"

Riley took a deep breath. "You know I don't like to tell you what to do."

This made a sip of water I'd just taken come out of my nose. "Um, yes you do!"

"Well, I'm rarely right. But I think, in this case, you just leap. Just take the leap."

"So if you were dating a guy and you weren't totally sure about anything, you'd just move in with him?"

"If the guy were Nick, yeah. In fact, if you don't do it, I might get a divorce and move in with him myself."

Just then, as if a bell to save me, I got another call. "Hold on a second, someone's calling."

"Just call me back. Love you!"

"Love you too!" I pushed the accept button for my new call without even looking. "Hello?"

"Beth, it's Lacey! Have I caught you at a good time?"

"Oh hi! Yes, of course! How are you?"

"I'm great and you're about to be too. I just booked us a gig in New York!"

"Are you serious? Where? This is amazing!"

"I sent a link to our stuff to a bunch of cool places and one wants us to play a weekend there. They're paying three grand, which we'll of course split equally. And they're even putting us up in a few rooms. We'll have to share. The only catch is, we have to pay our own flights. Are you up for it?"

Without even a second thought, I answered, "Of course I'm up for it! When?"

"That's the catch. It's actually the weekend after next. I know it's not a lot of notice, but I guess the band they had fell through or something. I've already looked at flights and there are some good deals to Newark. We'd have to leave on a Thursday. Can you miss a day or two of work?"

"I'm sure it won't be a problem. Oh shit, I'm nervous!"

"We'll be great! We're having rehearsal this Wednesday to go over the set list. Cool?"

"So cool! Thank you Lacey!"

"Thank YOU, Beth! You've brought the band good luck! I'll go ahead and book all our flights. Email me your legal name, birth date and passport number, ok? You can pay me or I'll take it out of your check at the end. See you Wednesday at our regular spot."

I hung up, in shock at how much life had changed in a matter of months. I figured I shouldn't question it too much. I'd just ride the amazing wave as it continued on its upward tick.

I called Riley back. "You won't believe this!"

"He asked you to marry him?"

"Shut up! No, better. Our band is playing in New York the weekend after next."

"Wow! That's so cool. You're going to be so famous! I'm gonna lose you to a world of cocaine and prostitutes. Please, don't go down that road."

Only half listening, I laughed. "I'm really excited for this. I've only been to New York once and it was when we were kids."

"I remember that trip well. You cried when we saw CATS. You thought they were going to abduct you."

"They really got all up in my space, remember?"

"I am so excited for you sweetie. This is just so cool for you! I wish I could go."

"Thank you! I feel like I have you to thank for this string of good things!"

"You only have yourself to thank. You're rocking it girl." She then covered the phone and yelled to Mark. "Honey, do you NOT hear the dryer buzzer? Jesus, do I have to do everything around here?" Back into the receiver, she said, "I have to run. The house is falling apart. So excited for you, love!" Click.

I knew I should call Nick in this moment, but I just wanted to sit in the stillness for a bit; let it wash over me before some other shoe somewhere dropped. Everything was truly coming up roses and I would allow myself to sniff them for awhile.

Chapter Twenty: Jack's Dream

A week went by and I hadn't heard anything back from Gero. I hoped this meant he had his nose buried in the case and was only one clue away from cracking it. Everything in London was plodding along: the gray sky, the cool showers, the hustle, the uncertainty. Stephen seemed to be adjusting somewhat to his new apartment, although the separation was extremely tough.

I asked him if I should reach out to Lydia to be polite. He gave me his blessing and luckily I received her voicemail as I was in no mood for a conversation. I told her I was thinking of her and hoping for the best. The truth is, I really missed the kids. I decided next time Stephen got them for the weekend, I'd come along.

On one particularly rainy Sunday, after I'd worked on a few legal briefs, I fell asleep on the couch watching cricket on the telly. I drifted in and out of REM sleep, all the while drooling on my T-shirt. But one dream especially stood out. I was standing at the foot of a bed, in some room I don't remember ever having seen. Suddenly, I felt a burst of warm air all over my body and Beth appeared from under the black silk sheets. She beckoned me to the bed so I climbed on top of her.

Dream Beth smelled as good as Real Beth and I began kissing her all over. Her skin was wet and her body as soft as my waking-self remembered. Only in the dream version, we didn't stop at "next time." I entered her and our bodies intertwined like a wave lapping at the shore. Moving in and then retreating and then in again just to see how far it could go. She moaned and then whispered, "Jack, wait for me."

I woke up covered in sweat and something else. Was it fear? Fear that I will never again experience anything as good as that night or that dream? Luckily the fear turned into determination. I told myself, tomorrow I will contact Gero again and if he can't help me, I'll find someone who can. I went back to sleep hoping to dream of her again, but she eluded me and instead my brainwaves skipped the REM cycle and went straight into dreamless deep sleep.

I slept hard and when I woke up, it was 5:00am. The sun had not yet risen, but I decided to make the most of my perfect sleep and get up anyway. Fiona had once suggested meditation, so I tried for about 30 seconds, but got frustrated by my never-ending thoughts so I stopped. I instead made some bacon and eggs, read yesterday's newspaper and did 20 sit-ups. I would have a good week if it were the last thing I would ever do. I had to remind myself that overall, I was a pretty happy person. True, the last year had been full of wanting and okay, a little desperation. But it was time to turn all of those ridiculous emotions into change for the better.

When I got to work, I shut the blinds in my office and called Gero. He answered on the fourth ring. "Yes?"

"It's Jack Stoll? We met last week about the American girl?"

"Oh yes, yes. I was going to call you today. I may have found her. Is it possible that she moved to a state called Iowa?"

I had no idea. "I guess anything is possible. What did you find?"

"I went through as many Beths from California as I could find on Facebook. One, who fits your physical description and age, now lists herself as living in Des Moines. But I might have some bad news. It appears she's newly married."

My heart ruptured. "No. I doubt it! No!"

Gero remained unmoved. "Stand by. I'm going to email you the photo and you tell me if this is her. I'll stay on the line with you."

I'm sure it only took him about 15 seconds to email the photo, but it felt like centuries. It popped into my in-box and so much of me didn't want to open it. If I just didn't know she was married and had moved on, I could continue this fantasy of how meant to be it all was. But my curiosity overruled my delusion and I clicked on the message and inhaled.

It took the photo a few seconds to load and I did not exhale the entire time. It started downloading at the top and I could see wisps of reddish brown hair. Could this be her? Next was a creamy white forehead. Oh no! Is it...? Then the whole picture finally loaded and this was clearly an older, heavyset woman in her 50s.

"Gero!" I happily screeched into the phone. "This woman is not in the age range I gave you! Why would you scare me like that?"

Gero seemed un-phased. "What do you mean? She looks late 20s to me."

"Maybe in Germany! But America, no. You're about 30 years off."

"Okay, I'll call you when I have another lead." He hung up without saying goodbye and I've never been happier for someone to fail at their mission.

Chapter Twenty-One:
On The Topic Of Love

I drifted through the next few days at work in a happy and nervous daydream. I had eventually called Nick the day I got the news that our band was playing in New York and he seemed elated. He insisted on taking me out that weekend to celebrate my upcoming stardom.

When Wednesday night rolled around, I actually felt confident when I showed up for rehearsal. Obviously, we were doing something right; we just had to keep doing it. The rest of the band seemed to feel in high spirits too.

Lacey appeared at the front of the room with a big bottle of not-so-expensive Champagne. "Ladies! We have our first real gig outside of California. I want to thank everyone for their hard work and commitment to The Girls of Summer. And I especially want to thank our newest member, Beth, for being so great and also being such a good luck charm." She popped the cork and let some of the bubbles spray on my head! We all screamed in delight and then put the red cups Lacey had given us out for our sparkling wine pour.

"Cheers! Here, here! To Beth! To all of us!" We drank, but I stopped before I got too buzzed.

Lacey then got serious. "Okay, so now for the details. We are booked on a red-eye a week from tomorrow night out of Sacramento, which means we will have to leave here no later than 3:00pm on Thursday. So make sure that works for everyone. Also, they've given us two rooms in some hotel in Times Square, so we'll have three of us in one, and two in the other." She then printed out some pieces of paper. "I've printed out a potential list of songs for each night of our gig. Look it over, tell me if you think we're missing anything."

We looked over the list, discussed some songs and then rehearsed the entire set. Champagne made everything sound just a little bit better and I felt so alive and good to be in my skin. Life was finally happening because of me, not to me and even though I couldn't predict the future, I felt more in control than I ever had.

And yet there was this lingering question in the ether. Did I want to move in with Nick? Did I love him yet? Would I ever love him? I knew he was waiting for an answer and I simply wasn't ready to give it to him just yet. What I did know was I really liked him. I knew when I was around him, I felt safe and at ease. There was a kindness and romanticism to Nick that was hard to question. But somehow, I didn't feel excited when I knew I was going to see him. Even in our first month, I always felt like I had the upper hand and this was foreign to me. Was this what real love was? Mostly equal adoration and respect? No games? No butterflies? Was it all too good to be true?

I went home that night sweeping these important questions under the proverbial rug so I could focus on just being in a good mood. I knew Nick would probably bring it up again when we were out that weekend, but I wasn't going to rush my answer.

****

Friday night, Nick suggested he cook for us rather than a big night out on the town. I was so tired from my long workweek and the exciting upcoming New York gig, I was thrilled by the suggestion. By the time I got to his place, he had already filled up the air with the most delicious smelling pasta sauce I'd quite possibly ever experienced. He had some old Bob Dylan playing and an open bottle of red wine on the counter, which he sipped as he cooked.

"Hi you!" he said when I opened his unlocked door. "Pour yourself a glass!"

"It smells so good in here. Wow! I think I will pour myself a glass."

"I'm so much cuter when you're drunk."

I poured my glass and kissed him on the cheek. His eyes crinkled so sweetly, as always, when he smiled back. He smelled like fresh fabric softener. "You're always cute!"

I sat in that moment and thought maybe I do love him at this exact time. And then the most interesting thought occurred to me about love in general. What if love wasn't something that you grew into, or out of? People were always falling in and out of love like it was some big, hot fiery pit you wanted to dip your body in and then escape. It was all so cliché. You meet, you get to know each other, and then one day: Oh I love him! Oh I love her! Then someone says it, and the other either reciprocates it or doesn't. If they do express reciprocity, the relationship progresses until one day, one of the parties escapes from the fiery pit. The other is left confused and swimming with the question, well what the hell do I do in this pit alone? As if the concept is just one big crescendo, which ultimately descends back down.

No. What if love is about moments? In this moment, I love him. In five minutes, I won't. In 10, I will. He made a joke and it made my heart sing and I love this. He didn't text me back; I don't love him right now. I don't mean to sound cynical, but it would seem that the healthiest kind of relationship is basing your love of another person on how they make you feel. And for most of us, this changes daily. Well, maybe not most of us. But the men I tend to date are quite unpredictable.

You can always care about another person. You can even remain loyal in your devotion to them. But love them every second of every day? That's insane. So maybe just then when Nick made the cute self-deprecating joke, I loved him. And maybe that was enough. But it was too hard and confusing to explain my new concept, so I didn't dare share the thought.

He finished cooking and we sat down on soft little red pillows to eat on the floor, Japanese style. "But we're eating Italian food?"

Nick nodded. "Yes, but how would we eat food in the style of the Italians? We have quick affairs with our mistresses and then a big family-style meal?"

"Hey, careful! I'm 1/16th Italian!"

"Aren't we all?" And I loved him.

He then laughed, which included a little snorting sound. And I didn't love him.

"Fair enough!" I conceded, as I took a bite of the delicious pasta.

"So how excited are you for New York?"

"I can't believe this is happening. Our band is good and all, but are we this good?"

"What? Of course! You're better! You should be playing at Madison Square Garden."

"Okay, easy buddy. Let's not go crazy."

"But seriously, you're really, really good."

His phone buzzed and he quickly looked at what I assume was a text. Out of character, I said, "Who's that?"

He seemed just a dash flustered. "Oh, no one. Stupid work thing."

He didn't often talk about work, so I was surprised to hear him complain. "They text you Friday nights now?"

"Sadly, yes. Ugh." He quickly texted something back and then threw his phone down on the couch behind us. "Now, let's just focus on our wonderful Italian slash Japanese meal." He paused for a moment. "Unless of course, you wanted to talk about, say, that question I asked you last weekend?"

I suddenly became very hot. "Oh yeah. About moving in, I haven't decided on that yet. I just really like my place but don't think it's big enough for both of us. And, I guess, I'm not opposed to making a big change. I just need time. I'm sure living with you would be awesome!"

His phone beeped again and this time he was receiving a call.

"Do you need to answer that?"

"No, they can go screw themselves. Sorry!"

I wondered if his sudden display of a previously unseen edge was a result of my indecision. I hoped not, but would understand it if it were the case. "Fair enough! Anyway, give me a little time, okay? I love being with you Nick. I know that."

"And I love being with you! But you already know this. Okay, let's watch a movie."

"Yes! And it's chef's choice tonight, so whatever you want."

We curled up into each other and let my lack of decision waft into the couch cushions, along with all the loose change and popcorn kernels.

Chapter Twenty-Two:
Time For A London Break

After my Spanish getaway with Stephen, I really started getting the itch to travel more. I was due at least three weeks of paid vacation from work, and life in London, although always quite interesting, was such a hustle. I needed to be "Holiday Jack," whom I always liked so much more than "Serious Jack." Don't we all like our holiday selves more?

After attending a lovely dinner party thrown by my friend Kate, I came home and started looking online for good airfare deals. Some man from the party whom Kate worked with was going on and on about how cheap vacation packages were and how he and his girlfriend just got back from a Turkish cruise. The only time someone else's holiday is tolerable to hear about is when you have hopes to experience one as well.

I clicked around a travel website, and of course the ad that caught my eye immediately was one for an all-inclusive package to California. There were plenty of New York deals as well, and they all seemed intriguing. I explored the idea of traveling to both coasts. Or perhaps a Turkish cruise instead? The world was my oyster, as they say, and I just needed to dig for the pearl.

I checked my voicemail and Stephen had left a message in which he sounded uncharacteristically upset. Not that this would be surprising, but he didn't often express emotion.

I decided that even though it was just past 11:00pm, I should call him back. "What's going on? Did I wake you?"

"Hi. No, I'm up. It was just an especially hard day with Lydia and the kids. She hates me so much and I'm afraid she's poisoning them to hate me too."

I fibbed slightly. "Lydia wouldn't do that. She knows better. And the children do too." Off his silence, I continued. "Is there anything you're not telling me about the separation? I know you said you'd been feeling distant for quite some time, but it really does seem quite sudden the whole thing."

I could hear Stephen take a sip of his drink. "No. We're just not in a good place. And I'm not sure we will ever get back there. But being in this in-between state is actually the worst because I can't go back and I can't move on. I suppose you understand where I'm coming from."

I'm fairly certain he was being violently sarcastic with this statement, but I chose to play ignorant. "Yes, yes. I do understand."

He cleared his throat. "Yes, it's totally the same thing."

Because he was feeling so blue, I decided to let his scathing commentary on my recent pain go unremarked upon. "Well, stiff upper lip as we say. What's next? What can I do to help?"

"For now, there's nothing, although I'm very grateful for you. I may have to steal you again soon for a getaway, but I'm not quite sure when. I don't ever want to miss a moment with the kids."

"Funny you should mention. I was just looking online for that exact same thing. Perhaps sooner rather than later, yeah?"

"Yes, please. Thank you again for listening to my nonsense. Good night!"

"It's not nonsense if we're related, now is it? Good night, sleep well. Tomorrow will be a better day."

"Let's hope!" We hung up and I felt some change in the air. Good or bad, it seemed as if I were on the precipice of something new and this pleased me.

Chapter Twenty-Three:
New York State Of Mind

Packing for New York is especially difficult when 70 percent of your clothing must be 80s-inspired. I threw in big pink skirts and hair-bows and black, rubber bracelets and lace gloves. It was supposed to be pretty rainy and cold, so I tossed in some sweaters and scarves too. We were only going from Thursday to Monday night, but I never could bring just one or two pairs of shoes, and I wasn't even a shoe addict, like many of my friends. There needed to be rain-boots and snow boots and at least one pair of cute heels. The 80s Jellies flats (which I was able to score two pairs of at a vintage clothing shop) packed in easily. But there was also the crimping iron, the hair mousse, the giant bag of brightly colored eye shadow.

Lacey had given us a lecture about really committing to our decade's theme. She said at our last meeting, "We're like the band KISS, but without the business smarts of Gene Simmons or anyone dressed as a cat."

My boss was surprisingly cool about me taking time off and even let me stay home Thursday morning to ensure I wouldn't feel rushed. We all met at Alyssa's house as she had a huge SUV to drive us (and our instruments) to the Sacramento airport. The trip went by quickly as we sang and told stories and best of all, we laughed in that way that girls can do only when no boys are around. It was heavenly.

The trip itself was not quite so pleasant, as there were rain delays and middle seats and crying babies. But eventually we arrived in Newark, and made our way through the thick yet cold air to Times Square. Our hotel looked exquisite from the lobby, but we were sad to find out the rooms themselves were not quite on par. We were so tired by the time we hit the beds, however, it didn't even matter.

Lacey and I took one room and the other three girls took the other, with Alyssa opting for the cot because it was "better for her back." I fell asleep before I could even brush my teeth, but as tired as I was, I still had thousands of butterflies, as we'd be taking the New York stage the next day. I slept deeply, despite Lacey's snores, which could saw a tree in half.

****

Even though I was up by 8:00am, I had to wait until at least 11:00am New York time to check in with Nick and Riley back in California. Riley seemed even more ecstatic than I was about our gig that weekend, but then again, like any good sibling, she was always more supportive of me than I was of myself. Nick was sleepy when I called and though he sounded happy to hear from me, I detected a bit of an edge to his voice. I didn't have time to decipher it at that moment, as we had rehearsal at the club at noon.

We went over our attire and set list for the evening, and then we all decided that 1:00pm was not too early to have a beer. I let the energy of New York sweep over me, carried by honking horns and screaming construction workers and dreamy, hopeful artists. This city ignited something in me that I felt had been dormant in my sleepy California town. But it also scared me how fast it made my blood flow, like my veins couldn't quite keep up.

"Okay ladies," Lacey said authoritatively after we'd finished a round. "It's naptime. We need to be downstairs in the hotel lobby by 5:15 and at the club no later than 6. I hear traffic is unpredictable, so don't be late! We are gonna rock the East Coast, am I right?"

We all cheered and shuffled back to our respective hotel rooms. Lacey fell asleep almost immediately, while I stared at my phone and then the ceiling and then a muted TV for two hours. At 4:00pm, it was time to shower and get dressed for our big night. This was it. Or maybe not. Maybe it was just another night in the thousands of nights we would hopefully have on this Earth. Maybe all I had to do was breathe and live in the present and remember, this is supposed to be fun.

By the time we got to the lobby, I was really excited. We all looked amazing and glittery and fluorescent, as any good 80s cover band would. But en route to the club, my excitement turned to utter fear. When we finally arrived, I actually thought I might throw up.

The owner had a grey beard and was wearing very tight jeans. "You chicks look hot. I feel like I'm reliving my 30s, man. Those were the best times." He continued to ruminate about his yesteryears, but I tuned out. It was all I could do to keep breathing. We set up instruments, warmed up our voices and did our fake prayer circle a la Madonna circa her "Truth or Dare" tour. The time had come. The time was now.

****

From backstage, we could hear what sounded like a loud, blustery crowd out front. The club was aesthetically stripped down, with cement floors, dark lighting and lots of old black-and-white photos on the wall depicting other bands, both famous and not. There were two bars, one in the back of the room and one down the side, both stocked to the brim with extremely attractive bartenders waiting to make us sound better.

An emcee, a 20-something guy with a goatee, took the stage and asked the crowd if they were ready to rock "80s-style." A few people whistled. He asked again, "I SAID, are you ready to rock 80s-style? Because our first band tonight are some of the cutest, coolest, raddest, most awesome, totally 80s chickies around. At least that's what my boss told me to say. Anyway, they're here from California, so let's please put our hands together and give a New York City warm welcome to: The Girls of Summer!"

The crowd clapped, some harder than others, and we took the stage. I gave Lacey a "please talk first" look and, as usual, she was able to pick up on my panic. She blew into her mic. "Hello New York City! We're Girls of Summer and we want to take you back, all the way back to a time when girls just wanted to have fun!"

A few more people whooped it up, clapped or whistled. It wasn't an especially excited crowd, but they were at least being polite. I realized it was my turn to talk. "Yeah, get ready to dance people. I know we will!" I looked back at the band and gave them the cue to get started and suddenly Cyndi Lauper-inspired synthesizers and that hollow, specifically 80s drumbeat began.

Then I started to sing, and I once again transformed into everything I wanted to be. Eyes closed, voice en pointe, happy-go-lucky, Holly Go-lightly. And the crowd bought it! From Cyndi to Madonna to the Go-Gos, we even threw in a few male-band covers like Wham's "Wake Me Up Before You Go Go" and Duran Duran's "Hungry Like the Wolf."

But then we got to Prince. The group had debated on whether to play "Purple Rain," as it didn't really fit our "brand" as this happy, girlie group. But after taking it to a vote last week, majority of three (including me) to two won. It wasn't an easy tune to play on the guitar either, but we simplified some of the riffs to synth chords and decided to go for it!

This song had always made me emotional, but there was something about standing on that stage singing those heartfelt words that actually made tears form. When I got to the lyrics, "I never wanted to be your weekend lover," I became the words inasmuch as a person could become lyrics. Cheesy? Sure, but the idea of wanting something permanent, real, secure and passionate resonated so deeply with me through that one sentence, I was overwhelmed with emotion. I sang the next line, "I only wanted to be some kind of friend," and at that moment I opened my eyes and looked out into the crowd. There, standing in the center of the room amongst the party girls, beefy men, 80s enthusiasts and tourists was the unmistakable and glorious face of Jack.

****

For what seemed like light years, the Earth stopped spinning. I knew the song continued to fall out of my lips. I knew I was still breathing, still standing. But that was all I knew. Nothing else made sense. When the song finally got to its guitar solo, I turned to Lacey and mouthed, "bathroom break." She nodded, albeit with a concerned look, and I walked back stage to put my head between my legs.

When they finished, I heard Alyssa announce we would take a short break. The crowd at this point was pretty into us, it seemed, and they let out a delicate roar. The other women came back to the greenroom where I was chugging water and wiping up my sweat.

Lacey put her arm on my shoulder. "Great job everyone! Beth, are you okay? You cool?"

"Yeah, I just think I … I saw a ghost."

Alyssa perked up. "A real ghost? I knew there was something haunted about this place!"

I laughed, I think. "No, a guy. A person I met overseas who disappeared and is now, somehow, here."

I realized I'd never told the group about my affair with Jack. I wanted the band to represent a new chapter, the future. I didn't want to hold onto an obsession that seemed impossible to resolve.

The girls began to bombard me with a litany of questions until Lacey intervened. "Let's talk about this later, girls. We've got to get back out there. Beth? You ready?"

"As I'll ever be," I said, half meaning it.

We walked back out and the crowd cheered. Before the light hit my eyes and I could actually still make out the people in the audience, I scanned the crowd, partly expecting Jack to be gone. I figured it had to have been some sort of mirage created by my mind out of a need to repair the confusion that still seemed to be blocking me from moving on.

Not only was Jack still there, he had moved closer to the stage. We locked eyes for a moment and I could hear my neurons scrambling to make sense of it. Our next song was "Missing You" which had always buried itself into my softest memories. The lyrics "Down this long-distance line tonight" had even struck a chord in me as a child. The idea of love traveling a far distance away from me, with no explanation as to why, was always heartbreakingly chilling.

I got through the song without crying, but I kept my gaze in Jack's direction. We played a few more songs and the crowd seemed even more excited as we went along. To say the whole thing was serendipitous would be an understatement. Go overseas, meet a guy who changes my life only to have him vanish. Take that change and allow it to inspire me to follow my dreams, said dreams lead me back to the guy. It's all so insane and yet, sure. Why not?

We went back to the greenroom after the show ended and I said to no one in particular, "I have to get out there, before he leaves again."

Lacey asked, "Do you want us to go with you?"

"No. Sure. Wait, no. I guess it doesn't matter."

"Here." She handed me a vodka tonic. "Maybe take a sip."

I did and then headed out into the main room. I saw Jack at the bar with his back turned away from me. I inhaled deeply and tapped him on the shoulder.

He turned around. "Hello? Great job up there by the way!"

"Jack? It's me, Beth! Remember the woman you left alone at the Tube station in London? Don't you recognize me?"

He visibly looked like he had just swallowed air. "Oh my Lord. You're Beth. You're her. Hi Beth! I'm not Jack. I'm actually his brother, Stephen. You have no idea how happy I am to meet you!"

Chapter Twenty-Four:
The Phone Call

It was 4:00am when my phone rang. Exhausted and disoriented, I looked to see it was a call from Stephen so I knew I should answer. "What's wrong? Are you okay?"

"I'm more than okay, mate! Get ready for this!"

I knew he'd wanted to get out of dodge for a bit and had settled on the States. I really had wanted to join him, but he oddly picked a weekend he knew I had to work. Perhaps he just needed time alone. He sounded pretty blasted. "Are you still in New York?"

"I am, and I'm sorry to call so late. But I think you'll want to hear what I have to say!"

I was exhausted. "Go on, then."

"Wait, I'll let you talk to her yourself."

I heard some static and what sounded like a mobile phone being fumbled about. Then I heard a nervous-sounding female voice. "Jack, is that you?"

"It is; who is this?"

"It's Beth. You know, Beth from California? We met in London a few…"

I cut her off with excitement. "Beth! THE Beth! How can this be?"

"It just so happens that your brother wandered into the New York pub in which my band was playing!"

This couldn't really be happening. The voice, her voice, traveling in bits and pieces, bouncing in packets of sound waves off satellites. Beautiful, orbiting satellites so close to crystal-like stars. It all brought Beth to me at the speed of sound, which was much too slow and yet I was never more thankful for NASA. Or mobile phones. "Your band? You live in New York now? This is amazing. Beth, I have to tell you what happened. You have to know … "

"Your brother told me. You fell outside the Tube station in the snowstorm. Please know I didn't leave you there. I couldn't find you! I looked everywhere!"

"Beth … I …"

"You poor baby! He told me you had to go the hospital. You must have wondered where I was!"

"I was so worried. I can't believe I'm talking to you. I can't believe you're there with my brother and not me. I know this is crazy, because we only knew each other for two days, but I've missed you! I've tried to find you."

"Jack, you have no idea. This year has been insane. I thought maybe I dreamt the whole thing."

"If I buy you a ticket, will you please come to London?"

She fell silent for what seemed like an eternity, but was probably only five seconds. "I … I …"

And then it dawned on me that maybe she had moved on. Why wouldn't she? Perhaps I'd concocted this whole love story in my mind and to her, it was just two fun evenings on holiday. Had I gone mad? But I couldn't allow my self-doubt to cloud this phone call. I had waited too long for this moment and I didn't want to mess it up. "No worries, just I'm so glad to hear your voice. Please, tell me your phone number so I can find you again. And your last name!"

She gave me her number and then said, "It's Wilton. Beth Wilton."

I rolled the name around in my mind. "Beth Wilton. Yes. Of course." I said it again. "Beth Wilton. It's so good to hear your voice!" I didn't want to hang up the phone, but suddenly it got very loud on her end. "Beth? Can you still hear me?"

"Jack, I think my phone is going. Jack? Are you still there? Listen, I can't hear you but if you can still hear me, I got all of your information from your brother. I will call you soon, okay? It's so lovely to…" And then the phone went silent.

The thought of going back to sleep was hilarious. I lay awake and stared at the ceiling, my hope in the universe fully restored.

Chapter Twenty-Five:
Breathe, Beth, Breathe

What do you do when everything you thought you'd figured out gets turned upside down on its head? Jack was alive. He was a plane ticket away. And just hearing his voice confirmed to me that no, this was not some fluke, vacation kind of fling. There was something very real there, beyond just the electrical charges and the chemistry. Something about him opened a door in me that led to the woman I want to be. It was all so crazy, but now I knew my feelings were real.

But I had real feelings for Nick too. I'd built a mini world with him and even though I had my doubts, I really cared about him. My head told me to move in with him, continue down this road in the town I'd always known. Stay the course, be practical, work hard. But my heart? It wanted me to take flight. Now the question was: which one do I listen to?

First things first, I'd call Riley! I had come back to the room in a bit of a daze, unsurprisingly. Lacey had gone out after the show, so I had the whole place to myself. The high of the great show (mixed with a vodka tonic or two) was nothing compared to Jack's voice. I was almost too excited to dial, but somehow I managed. She answered immediately.

"Hi! How'd the show go, rock star?"

"The show was great but that's not why I'm calling."

"Oh, let me sit down for this. What's up? Are you tipsy?"

"Not really. Not anymore. First how are you?"

"Beth, tell me!"

"Okay, so I'm singing a song and I look out into the audience and Jack is there."

She literally screamed into the phone. "What? Are you … what?"

"So after the show, I go up to him, obviously and I say hello. And it turns out, it's not Jack, it's his twin brother Stephen!"

"This is way, way better than even *The Young and the Restless*!"

"I know, right?"

"Next you'll tell me he got abducted by aliens!"

I laughed. "Anyway, so I'm completely freaking out! And at first I thought, what if this is really Jack and he doesn't want to deal with it, so he's made up this twin brother?"

"I swear to you that thought crossed my mind."

"Well it turns out, no, because he then called Jack back in London, even though it was like 4:00am there. And we talked!"

"I can't breathe! Are you serious? What did he say? Did he tell you why he disappeared?"

"Actually, before we called him, his brother told me everything. Apparently, when we had to be outside of the subway during that storm, he fell. I didn't see it because the visibility was so bad with the snow and people. But he was knocked unconscious! He had to go to the hospital and everything and the whole time, he thought I left him there!"

"I am so glad I answered this phone call. This is just … wow. Do we believe this?"

"Of course we believe it! Riley, it was incredible to hear his voice. It answered so many questions. But of course, it raised a lot of questions too. Like what am I supposed to do? What do I choose?"

"Obviously, I've never met Jack but you know how much I love Nick. And he's been pushing so hard to win you over. Wow, you hit a dry spell for years and now you're wanted by men on every continent!

"I'm sorry, what men want me in Antarctica? Or Africa, Asia or South America for that matter?"

"Let's not get lost in the details. So what are you gonna do?"

"I think I need to call Nick. I need to be honest with him about what's happening."

"Before you even know what you're going to do?"

"I think so, yes. Let me call him before it gets too late. Okay? I love you!"

"Love you. But Beth? Follow your heart, okay? It won't steer you wrong."

But that was just the problem. In my past, my heart or my gut or the neurons firing fero-ciously in my brain, always did seem to steer me wrong. Sure we can all say everything is just a life lesson and there are no wrong answers. Everyone is on this earth to teach us and help guide us in the direction we're meant to be going. But is that really true? For example, me accepting a date with an alcoholic, semi-homeless juggler in my early 20s whom I'd met in a park, was there really a life lesson there? Or was I just attracted to the strange, tortured, nomadic "artist"? (To be fair, we only went out once.) I guess my point is that I didn't trust my decisions. But my heart was certainly speaking loudly on the matter.

I decided to Skype Nick, as I really wanted to see his face. He didn't answer, but my cell phone rang a few minutes later when he called me back.

"Hi," he whispered. "I'm with some friends but wanted to make sure I talked to you! How was it?"

"The show was great! We had so much fun and the audience seemed to eat it up." I felt so guilty for my omission of all the facts. "Which friends are you out with? Are you having fun?"

He paused. "Oh, I don't think you know these ones. I should probably get back inside the restaurant, but I'm so glad it went well. I knew it would!"

We hung up and I felt full of self-doubt. As everyone had pointed out, Nick was the real deal, the full package. And still, something was holding me back. Something even other than Jack and I couldn't quite put my finger on it. But as I'd said before, I tended to have failings in the "picking" department. My instincts had not served me well in the past.

I wanted to call Jack back, but thought I'd give it a little time first. I didn't want to be tipsy or tired when I settled in for a phone call. I fell asleep, equal parts confused and excited. Jack, Jack, Jack. He was real. And after all this time trying to find him again, I had acci-dentally gone and made a life for myself.

****

I woke up around 10:00am, still blurry-eyed, but unable to sleep. I made myself a cup of coffee and even though I know it's not the highest quality, there's nothing better than vacation/hotel coffee in the room. I never really understood why but I figured it was the same reason hotel bathrobes felt softer too.

Lacey stumbled in around 11:00am, making no excuses for what seemed like a pretty wild night. "Hi!"

"Hey party girl! I was getting worried!"

"I called up some old college friends and they showed me what New York really looks like. Turns out it doesn't get going until about 3am."

"I wish I could keep up with all that. Back home, I'm usually asleep before 10."

Lacey giggled. "I know, me too! Isn't this gig FUN?! Oh by the way, me and the girls are meeting in 30 minutes for brunch. Are you in?"

"I think I'll just keep resting. Last night was kind of crazy for me."

She started putting on moisturizing face lotion. Then she sprayed some deodorant on and changed shirts. "Oh yeah — whatever happened with that English guy?"

"It's too long of a story. But I promise I'll fill you in!"

"Okay champ!" She sprayed herself with some perfume and grabbed her keycard once again. "I'm off! If you're not here when I'm back, we're meeting at the club for tonight's show at 7. Everything should be the same as before, except I'm writing up a new set list so we switch it up a bit."

"Sounds good," I said, rolling back over onto the pillow.

After staring at the ceiling for 10 minutes I finally got out of bed, got coffee-d up and stared at the phone number for Jack that his brother had put it into my cell. I did a quick calculation to determine that if it was 11:30 in New York, it was 4:30pm UK time. Perfect, I figured. Maybe some of it was the caffeine, but my heart was racing so hard and fast that I thought maybe I was having some sort of attack.

I counted to three out loud and then yelled "Go," at which point I hit: "Call Jack." There was a brief pause and then that double ring you get when calling England. "Ring ring. Ring ring. Ring ring." Was he really not answering? One more double ring and then voicemail. "Hello, you've reached Jack Stoll. I'm away from my mobile but please do me the honor of leaving a message, and it shall be my pleasure to ring you back." Every single word melted my heart. So much so that my words dissolved from the heat of his voice into a pile of nothingness. In other words, I couldn't speak.

I hung up, a bit surprised that he hadn't been simply waiting by the phone. I realized it might have seemed weird not to leave a voicemail, but I just couldn't do it. I figured he would see that I'd called and call me back in no time.

But then I thought, what if he didn't see it? After all this time, I finally had his number and I'd told him I would call. I felt insane but hit redial anyway. Again, I waited through a few double rings and his beautiful outgoing message and this time, I mustered up the courage to speak. "Hi there, um, Jack. It's Beth, you know from California. Well, in New York now, but, well, in the United States of America." Oh dear. I was losing it. "Anyway, it was amazing to hear your voice last night and I thought I'd try you. And well, hi and cheerio and all that!" Worst message ever. I hung up and hoped it didn't sound as awkward as it clearly did.

I showered and went for a New York stroll, past delis and vintage clothing stores. The hustle of Times Square was exciting and terrifying at the same time. I decided to Uber to the Upper West Side for a little jaunt at the Natural History Museum. I'd never been but had seen plenty of Woody Allen movies and this seemed like the perfect, romantic place for self-reflection. Plus, it was pretty cool!

As I sauntered past dinosaur bones and the air-conditioned caveman reenactments, my mind raced in a thousand directions. Nick, the show, work. But it always came back and settled on Jack. I wondered what it would be like to have him by my side. Would we stare in awe at the saber-toothed tigers? Would we kiss under a constellation in the planetarium? Or would it turn out we had nothing to say to each other? That our connection had been purely a result of my being a damsel in distress in the romantic London snowfall?

I guess some of those questions could be answered, if only he'd call me back.

I stopped for a quick bite at the overpriced cafeteria and enjoyed the next few hours searching every nook and cranny of the museum, all without looking at my phone. This was quite a feat and I was proud and happy to get lost in the darkness of fossils and screaming children.

When I finally did check the time, I was surprised to see it was almost 5:00pm! I had to hustle back down to the hotel, change into my 80s gear and get to the club downtown. Still no word back from Jack, or Nick, for that matter, but I figured people have their own stuff going on. Once, in therapy, Allison told me to remember that none of us are the stars of other people's lives. We're all co-stars at best so we shouldn't expect anyone's full attention, really ever. This was both sad and comforting at the same time.

I got back to the room and I was happy to see that Lacey was still there. We talked a bit about our day, sidestepping my big "did I talk to the English guy" question. Although in keeping with Allison's theory, Lacey might not have even remembered. She had her own life, after all, which she oddly didn't talk much about.

We met up with the rest of the girls in the hotel lobby once again and made our way to the club. This time the nerves were way less noticeable. We went over the new set list, had a cocktail and waited for show time, which was at 8:30.

At 8:15, one of the bartenders came into the greenroom. "Which one of you is Beth?"

Surprised, I raised my hand like I was in 5th grade. "I am?"

"I have a note for you." He handed it to me and disappeared back into the front of the club.

The girls oohed and ahhhed and began chanting, "Beth got a note, Beth got a note."

Lacey reminded me, "You'd better open it quickly, because we're on in two minutes."

Logic told me it was probably from Jack's brother. Anyone else would just call me. My hands were shaking as I opened it and read: "Hi Beth. Hope you have a great show tonight. I'll be watching from the front row. Love, Jack."

The blood from my veins rushed to the very top of my head. "It's … from … him," I said out loud to the room. "It's Jack. He's, he's here."

One of the stagehands popped in at just that very moment. "Okay girls, it's show time! Let's go!"

Before I had a chance to process anything, we were whisked onto the stage in the darkness, where I grabbed on to the microphone for dear life.

Chapter Twenty-Six:
First Flight Out

So often, when it's really early in the morning, our minds don't always conjure up the best decisions. Perhaps we convince ourselves out of exhaustion that we can skip that morning's exercise or breakfast in favor of just a few more minutes of sleep.

This was not the case on this particular morning. The second I hung up from Beth, I leapt out of bed to grab my laptop. After a quick search of flights from Heathrow to any New York City airport, I was shocked to find a last-minute deal for less than 500 quid. It left London at 10:00am, arriving at JFK around 3:00pm which gave me more than enough time to get packed and to the airport.

As I stared out the plane window at the clouds, I wasn't even the tiniest bit nervous. Even if Beth had moved on, even if she wasn't overjoyed to see me after all this time, I was going to see her. And there was no way I was going to allow my cynical mind to spin that negatively.

Tom Petty's "American Girl" came on and I smiled the rest of the trip, as I sipped my beer and continued looking for patterns in the clouds.

****

Got to New York with no delays and immediately called my brother, who had encouraged me to come. Not that I needed his encouragement, but he seemed more excited for my reunion with Beth than he was for his own marriage. He told me where to meet him and he'd already booked a room for me for two nights at the same hotel.

"You seem awfully jolly," I said once I arrived, meeting him in the hotel lobby, a bit jet-lagged.

"This is going to be a good night. You're right about that Beth girl. She's pretty special. Also, I have other good news! Come on, let's get you checked in."

"Oh what's the good news?" I asked, while simultaneously greeting the woman at check-in and handing over my passport.

"Lydia and I are getting back together!"

"That is fantastic news! Oh that genuinely pleases me!" Even though Lydia wasn't my all-time favorite, I had to concede that Stephen was much happier with her and even triple the happiness being at home with his children. Because we're twins, I often feel that his triumphs are my own.

"Yes, agreed. I'll fill you in but first, let's focus on your big reunion!"

"I don't know what's stopping me from actually calling her now. Maybe I should rather than surprise her at the show?"

"No. You must keep this lovely 'Affair to Remember' romantic thing going."

"Perhaps. But just so you know, that's not the best reference to our love story. Things didn't work out so well for them."

"You know what I mean! Now go up to your room and nap. You're going to need it for tonight. The show starts at 8:00 and it's at some awful, strange warehouse in the East Village. Very 80s, which I suppose was on purpose, because they're an 80s band."

"How did she look? My Beth? Was she kind to you?" I realized I hadn't asked these questions earlier. After we'd all hung up, I was booking my flight and in a mad dash for Heathrow.

"She's very pretty. And she seemed really happy and confused by the whole thing. But mostly happy! Can you believe it? I found her for you!"

"I owe you big time, brother!"

"Yes you do. You can start when we get back by helping me move my stuff back into my home."

"Consider it done. Going to my room. Shall we meet down here for a quick bite before the show at say 6:30?"

"Sounds ideal. Cheers!"

We went to our respective rooms where I lay on the bed, unable to sleep. Instead I listened to the voicemail Beth had left me while I was flying — oh, about 20 times. I wanted so badly to call her, to see her right away, to kiss her, to touch her. But I figured we'd waited this long, not by our own doing, and what was a few more hours if it meant a more romantic encounter?

I stared at the hotel room ceiling, my mind racing. I'll just listen to this voicemail one more time...

****

Stephen and I grabbed a quick "Reuben" sandwich, this enormous, American pile of meat and other items stuck between giant, oversized slices of bread. Delicious. He told me that he and Lydia started talking about three weeks ago, and slowly but surely, they decided he would move back in and they'd give it another round. I was genuinely supportive, of course, but had a tough time even paying attention to his words. In less than two hours, I'd see her again. All this searching and waiting and wondering and pining was finally going to come to an end.

We got to the club at 7:45. It was pretty crowded, with a mix of old 80s looking punkers and shiny young millennial types. I hadn't yet had time to exchange my pounds for dollars, so Stephen plopped down 30 bucks for our tickets. New York wasn't cheap, that was for sure. But I'd have paid 1,000 pounds to be here!

Once inside, I scoured the sticky floors and humid air for any trace of her. There was a lightness to the room, just knowing she'd been in there and would soon be again. Stephen bought us a couple of pints and as I drank mine, I never stopped scanning for a sighting. Then, to the left of the stage, I saw a door marked "Green Room." I could no longer take her absence.

"Steve, I'll be right back."

He half-answered, "Right you are," and went about drinking his lager.

As I walked toward the door, the very piece of painted wood that I assumed separated me from the woman I'd longed for, I outstretched my arm and just as I was about to turn the copper knob that stood in the way, a large man stepped in front of the door.

"May I help you?" He asked, his New York accent echoing through the bare hallway.

"Oh I was just going to visit a friend before the show, if that's all right."

"Sorry, you can't go back there without permission. I can give someone a message for you, if you want?"

"Could I write one quickly?"

"Sure, but hurry."

I pulled a flyer someone had given me on the street from my coat pocket and asked the man if he had a pen handy. He seemed annoyed but oddly was able to comply. I wrote a quick hello to Beth and gave it to him. "Thanks, mate. That helps a lot!"

"No problem."

Despite his menacing look, I thanked him again and headed back out to the main room, my breath quick. I found Stephen, who had happened upon a few rugby players and was having a chat.

"Jack! These guys are from Manchester!"

We all said hello and then the lights of the club dimmed. A blue light came up and I was instantly reminded of the Beatles cover band Beth and I had seen together. A voice from a hidden DJ booth came booming onto a loud speaker.

"Ladies, gentleman, and everything in between!" The crowd roared. "Please, put your hands together for a very special treat we have tonight. All the way from California, and apparently 1984, it's the Girls of Summer. And let me tell you, they are definitely all that!"

Five shadowy hourglass figures walked onto the stage and took their places. I recognized Beth even in the darkness as she approached the front microphone and struck a pose. With only her silhouette as a reminder, I could remember every crevice of her body as we lay in that Savoy bed on that wintery day. Both then and now, I traced her with my fingers and waited impatiently for the lights to come on.

Chapter Twenty-Seven:
And Then He Was There

I could feel my sweat pulsing through my fluorescent-pink covered chest. The lights on the stage, so warm and bright, finally went on and like a pro, I robotically went into performance mode. "Hello New York City!" I screamed into the mic, mimicking what I've heard so many front men and women do in the past. "Are you ready to rock, 80s style?"

I couldn't quite make out any faces, as I was blinded by the stage lights, but I heard four drum clicks and I knew it was time to sing. This time, we started with Madonna's "Like a Virgin." There had been some talk of me writhing around the stage in a wedding dress, but I'd talked the others out of it.

Just as I got the chorus, a body in the crowd moved close enough to the stage that I could see the face attached to it. It was Jack, unmistakably, a face I had longed to see for a year. Next to him was his twin, and even though I only knew Jack's face for a few days so many months ago, I could tell who was who.

Jack looked at me with his cool eyes and warm smile. I held his stare for as long as I could while singing these silly Madonna lyrics. It was all I could do not to jump off that stage and into his arms. Or something like that. But I sang the song, and then another, and another. Jack never moved from the sweet spot he'd found where he'd beaten the light and won my gaze. Even when I looked around the room, I could feel his pupils on me, firing questions and heat.

In a million years, I would never have guessed this is how we'd have met again. I never thought any of it was possible. But I got to live in the sweat of these songs and the intensity of him watching me. I couldn't have choreographed this better if I tried. This far exceeded any fantasy I could have drummed up, any day.

Except! Just one minor detail. Life had happened along the way. Another heart had gotten involved and although I knew these kind of logical and very real facts to be true, they didn't register when Jack's lips curled upward toward a smile.

We finished our set and after two encores, took our final bows. I went backstage with the other girls and we congratulated each other on a weekend well done. "To many more gigs!" we toasted. I added, "That our real jobs will allow" and most everyone chuckled. I looked at my phone and was shocked to see I had 12 missed calls from Riley. I immediately panicked. Then I noticed I had one text from her too. I opened the message and it simply said: "Nick is there to surprise you. Why don't you answer your phone?"

The good news was that now I didn't have to worry about when I was going to talk to Nick. My decision had come to face me in person. I felt like a woman on one of those reality dating shows where she has to choose a mate in a big elaborate ceremony, while simultaneously getting rid of another mate. What a strange game we've made for ourselves. The modern-day gladiators, except instead of warriors, it was suitors. And it wasn't so much a matter of "May the Best Man Win" as it was "May the RIGHT Man Win."

Maybe if Jack and I had had more than a couple of days together, that spark would have faded into a lukewarm stagnation. Maybe if I'd met Nick in a romantic English setting, I'd be ruminating over him instead? Maybe it wasn't about the man himself, so much as it was about the circumstance in which I met them?

So I took five breaths and went out into the crowd. Through a sea of tall bar-hoppers and spilt beer, I searched for both my present and my brief past. Looking everywhere for eyes that knew me, I inched my way toward the bar. And then there he was. A man in a cashmere sweater was facing away but just by the way he stood, by the way he tilted his head ever so slightly to the left, I knew it was him. I knew it was Jack.

But I couldn't go to him – not yet, anyway. All this waiting, only to be separated by a glass pane of morality. I hoped he wouldn't see me just yet and I kept looking. I had to find Nick. I had to see if the heat I felt for Jack was felt for him too.

As my search became more and more frantic, I felt a hand on my shoulder. I turned around and Nick was there. Here we go.

Chapter Twenty-Eight: Nick's Version

I'm Nick Bailey and I'm originally from Portland. My friends, if forced to describe me, (and I'm not sure there's a scenario in which they'd be forced per se, but if they were) would say I was funny, easygoing and most of all loyal. I went to school at University of Oregon (Go Ducks!), I get along well with my parents and sister and I like being outside, although I'm not obsessive about it.

I also love the idea of being in love. I was always every girl's best friend in high school because I was just sensitive enough for them to tell me their boy problems, but I was funny and "boy-ish" enough for them to develop crushes on me. (Usually these crushes happened too late in our friendship to act upon.) And none of this happened out of manipulation. I genuinely respected and adored my friends, and wanted to see them all be happy.

I didn't find my first love until a few years after college. Her name was Laura and we met, of all places, at a park bench where we'd both stopped after vigorous runs. We dated for a year before we lived together for two. She was tall, with long, dark hair and bright green eyes. I loved her passion, determination, legs, heart, and toughness. She seemed very clear about what she wanted (and didn't want) out of life and she wouldn't settle for less than her vision.

Which brought us to my heartbreak. Just after our second year living together, we started talking about more serious matters: marriage, family, what we wanted out of life. Even though we were still young, these were the types of things that came up. When I found out that Laura, who'd always been on the fence when it came to "traditional" desires, felt adamant about not wanting children, I was devastated. It was never a question for me that I wanted a big family of kids. Or at least two. I was the Piggy Back King of my older sister's nephews. I was the guy who just wanted to grill some steaks outside while the family romped around in the pool.

I never felt embarrassed for wanting what some might call a "simple" life. To me, it was simply "life." There was nothing else. I begged Laura at the time to reconsider. I told her we were too young to know for sure. But she said she was sure and that although she loved me deeply, she couldn't hold me back from the dreams I had.

I felt like I loved her so much, that maybe I had it all wrong. Maybe my dreams were that of my parents or what society told me I was supposed to feel or have. I considered the fact that perhaps Laura was enough. Love like that didn't come along every day and when it did, maybe we were supposed to shift our plans to make it work. But it ultimately didn't matter because she made the decision for us. One day I'd come home from a weekend bike trip and she she'd packed up her stuff in a U-Haul. It was the middle of the day and she was crying. She pleaded with me to forgive her, but said she knew if she didn't leave, that we'd resent each other for the rest of our lives. And with that, she took her dishes and her blankets and whatever else and she split.

My heart deconstructed. I didn't think I could go on without her or that I'd even want to. I had always been a pretty positive, even-tempered person, but the depths to which my soul sunk that day could not be measured. I was a mess. I sat on the living room floor for three hours after she'd left. I couldn't move. I couldn't dial the phone. I couldn't even cry. Finally, after I'd scraped myself off the floor, I holed up in the bedroom that we'd shared together for at least a week until some college buddies came over and forced me to go outside.

Slowly, life became life again, but it really took time to heal. I finally found my footing again and after some soul searching, decided a change of scenery would be just what I needed. So I packed up and moved to California. First to San Francisco, and then after getting swallowed up in rent prices and hectic hippie hills, I applied for a job in a smaller town and have been here ever since.

It was my sister who heavily persuaded me to try online dating. She put the profile together and posted a few pictures she deemed handsome. (She called the pics approachable, which I guess is a compliment.) She picked the name "Union Jack" for me because she had just read a book about the Revolutionary War. She was strange that way. The problem was that no woman really caught my eye because they weren't Laura. Nothing made me want to "wink" at them or "like" their profile.

That is until I saw Beth. All that time I thought I'd been searching for another Laura and when I saw Beth's profile, I knew — or at least realized at the time — that what I really wanted was the opposite of Laura. Beth seemed quirkier, more city-like, funnier. Her smile was warm and so inviting and just something about the crimson strands in her hair — this pop of red in an otherwise safe, brown garden of beauty. I felt compelled to send her a message, so I did.

My love grew incredibly quickly. I never discounted the fact that I might have such strong feelings for her because she was less effusive than I was. Was her ambivalence what attracted me so much? Was I actually repeating a pattern? Whatever it was, it felt very strong and very real. Our first kiss was cool, like a rain shower in May. It was sweet and floral and, for me anyway, it opened something that had been closed for a long time.

I definitely moved faster than Beth. I was ready to tell her I loved her after a month, because I did. I wanted to spend every single moment with her, but I held back the best I could so as not to scare her. Until I could no longer hold back and then I went and told her everything I felt. She was kind in her response, but I could feel she was unsure. Despite her hesitation, I felt a certainty about her that even took me by surprise.

Which is why it was especially confusing when Laura called a month ago. We hadn't been in contact for over two years. I'd like to say the memory of her had faded, but that would be a lie. Our time together had created a pathway of neurons tunneled so deeply in my brain, they could not be disconnected. She was just in there and there was nothing I could do except recognize it and try to dance around it.

And it didn't mean I didn't love Beth too. Her sweetness was perfectly balanced by her sense of being a bit lost in life. Her sense of go-getting wasn't as intense as Laura's. She "go-got" by showing up, being funny, being loyal. I love that Beth was such a good, hard worker, such a kind sister, daughter and friend. She was feminine and smart and inquisitive and my feelings for her were never in question.

But Laura, even after all that time, was something altogether different. When she called on that Sunday morning, Beth had just left after one of our easygoing, fun dates. "Hi," she said. "It's me." And my throat dropped into my knees.

I didn't even pretend to not recognize her voice, but simply said. "Wow. Hi." I swear she could hear my heart pounding through the phone wires. "Where are you? How are you?"

I could hear her smile through the receiver. "I'm well. I'm actually living in Los Angeles now. I'm…Nick, I don't know if I'm allowed to say this but I miss you."

And there it was. Suddenly a door that had been closed, but not locked, became ajar. I didn't know what to do or say. "I'm surprised to hear this Laura. It has been so long."

"There are so many things I want to say to you, but I want to say them in person. I heard you were living not too far from me now. Do you think, would it be possible for me to come visit? I wouldn't stay with you or anything. I just want to talk to you face to face."

"I'm seeing someone now and I really care about her. So, you know, I've kind of moved on."

"I know I don't deserve it, but will you just hear me out? I respect that you're seeing someone. I don't expect anything to happen romantically. I just need to see you. But I understand either way."

Then suddenly I started laughing. It all seemed so funny to me in the strangest, most surreal way and I simply couldn't stop. My laughter made her laugh and hearing it — this sound of joy I hadn't heard from her in so long — reminded me how entrenched she was in my heart. "Ok. I guess it would be okay to see you. I do want to, I just want to stay respectful of everyone involved."

Without skipping a beat, she said, "I'll be there on Saturday and will call you then. I can't wait to see you Nick. I really cannot wait."

****

I went back and forth on whether to tell Beth that Laura was coming to town. She had her first big show with her new band at an Irish pub that Saturday night, so I decided it would be best to wait. Of course, I'd tell her eventually, but we hadn't been dating all that long and I didn't know the protocol. Plus, I didn't want to stress her out.

As she'd said she would, Laura called that Saturday morning from a hotel near downtown. She asked where a good place to meet would be and I told her about a coffee & sandwich place in between our respective locations. I expected to arrive first, but when I walked in, there she was. Her long hair, her long legs, her smile, all just shimmering like always as she sipped her coffee or whatever it was from a large, ceramic mug.

She saw me and stood up. "Hi. Thank you for … well, just hi."

"Hi." I stood there frozen. Do I hug her? Do I kiss her? Do we run away together? Of course the answer was no, except for the hugging part. We embraced, but I kept a slight physical distance between our chests, which would have otherwise naturally touched.

"You look great. You look like you."

"You too." I finally exhaled, somewhat dramatically. "Wow, Laura. This is such a surprise to see you. What are you doing here?" We both sat down and a waiter immediately came over and asked me what I wanted to drink. "Is it too early for vodka?" We all laughed and I ordered a latte.

"I'm here to see you. And again, I know this is crazy and I hope you will just hear me when I say I'm not here to disrupt your life or upset you. I've just had a lot of time to think. And I've wanted to see and tell you so many things for so long. And I just couldn't not see you anymore."

"You could have sent an email. Or a message. This is awfully dramatic, Laura, especially for you. I thought you didn't like drama." My latte arrived and I blew on it to cool it off.

"I know, but you know me. Go big or go home. It's just, being out there in the world without you, I realized, I was lost. All this time, I was never really happy. And then about a year ago, I was at a BBQ and there were all these kids around and I liked it. And I started imagining what it would be like if one of those kids looked like you and me. I started crying and you know that's not like me. To cry when there's beer around! But I realized maybe I did want kids. And if that was the case, there was no one in the world I'd want them with, but you."

A flood of beautiful emotion overtook me and I was relieved, validated, bittersweetly devastated, and shocked all at the same time. But I held it together and simply said, "Laura. Wow." After a long, strange pause, I added, "Like I said, I'm seeing someone now and she's special to me. In fact I haven't felt this much for anyone since, well, since you. And I feel disloyal even having coffee with you right now, if I'm being honest."

"I would never want to get in the way of you with another woman, if you really love her. I just needed you to know how I felt, okay?"

It's funny how you can believe you've come so far after a person breaks your heart. You cry and party and write and swear off dating and eventually, bit by bit, day by day, you find your footing again. You say something clever, you laugh, you eat ice cream. A month or a year goes by and you realize, "I didn't even think about her/him today until just this moment." You can stalk them on Facebook again without feeling sick to your stomach. "Okay, that's a cute baby" you'll say as you sift through their online photo albums. "I mean if that's what they wanted all along!"

You start re-entering the world you once knew together. This restaurant, that bar, this European city! And then the second you see their name in print in an email or hear their voice on the phone, it all comes crashing down again. Sure, you're steadier than you once were, but this isn't enough to keep you from keeling over.

Hearing these words and seeing Laura's face made me, in a sense, keel over. I'd waited so long for her to realize it was wrong to leave. And now there was someone else who might even be better for me! Who might love me back in the way I deserved. "I just need time to think, okay? I'm really into this other woman and I need to see where that goes."

Laura, a woman who didn't often cry, had a quivering lip. "I understand. I'm going back to L.A. You have my cell and stuff now if you want to call. I hope you do, but I understand either way."

We hugged again and this time, she held on a little longer. I decided it best to not lay this on Beth before her first big show. I convinced myself that there might not be anything to lay on her anyway.

****

As a little more time went by, I threw myself into everything other than the thought of Laura: work, friends, my soccer league, and of course, Beth. My feelings for her genuinely began to grow until I felt I might burst. I decided the whole dichotomy was ridiculous. Laura had her chance and I had moved on. I was going to give Beth every single ounce of me and see if it was enough.

Or at least this what I told myself I would do. I decided it was a great time to tell Beth how much I cared for her. And that it was quite possibly time to take it to the next level. If we were really to see if this thing had legs, we had to keep walking. Of course it wasn't lost on me that I was maybe pushing quickly so as to prove to Laura — or myself — that I was over her. I wanted to forge ahead with Beth to protect my heart from the past. But this realization didn't mean that what I felt for Beth wasn't real. It only confirmed that it had all become very, very confusing.

 And then one night, at dinner with Beth, I went for it. I told her I loved her and suggested we move in together. I knew it probably sounded rushed, but I stood behind my words as they truly supported my feelings. As feared, she seemed flattered but did not say "I love you" back. With regard to moving in, she at first completely lost her words and then finally said she'd have to think about it. I guess that was a better reaction than her throwing wine in my face and running for the hills. (Although, how strange would that be?)

The night after my big "love, let's move in" reveal, Beth found out she got a gig in New York and it was coming up quickly, which was a very big deal. And since the universe seemed hell bent on making my life extra dramatic, on that same day, Laura called again.

She wanted to talk one more time. I told her no, that it just didn't feel right. She said she understood, but that she wasn't happy about it.

Of course, though I tried, I couldn't stop thinking about the quiver in her voice or the way her hands looked as they rested nervously on the café table. I didn't want to think about these things, but they crept in like ninjas, all-powerful and stealth-like. I went for a long bike ride and probably sent Beth too many congratulatory texts, but I wanted to distract myself from going down the rabbit hole.

The distractions didn't work. And the fact that Beth hadn't yet agreed to live with me made me feel unstable and unsure about everything. Too many options. Too many splintered-off pieces of my heart bouncing spastically in a vacuum. Too much love, too many people to rest the love in. Good problem to have, I realized, but when you're in it and you're scared of making the wrong choice, it can be debilitating.

So I froze. Well, figuratively of course. I continued working hard and hoping the right answer would simply appear to me like a vision. As Beth was preparing to go to New York, I was preparing for some insight. But none of it came.

It was almost as if Laura creepily knew exactly when Beth left on Thursday, because the very next night, she showed up with a "knock, knock, knock" at my door. Had it been anyone else, I'd have been annoyed and a tad bit terrified. But it was Laura and so I was intrigued and now, even more confused than ever.

"You can't come in. I told you I'd call you if and when I was ready, but Laura ..."

"I know you still feel something for me. I could tell by the way you looked at me when I saw you last week. I also know you're a really good guy, one of the many reasons I love you. If you can look me in the eye and tell me you don't love me, I swear I won't keep doing this. Something in me has gone crazy and I think it's the fact that I'm certain we're meant to be together."

My mind was silently screaming, of course you love her. This kind of thing never truly goes away. But I couldn't say that. I couldn't say anything for 30 seconds. Finally, I lied. "I don't love you, Laura. I have moved on. Please respect that."

She stood in front of me, her eyes pleading. "I'm sorry. I shouldn't have come here again. I'm sorry I hurt you back then. I'm sorry for everything."

As I was about to speak again, my Skype feature rang with Beth's ringtone. "I have to take that. But don't leave. I don't want you to be so upset. Can you meet me at the Rose Bar on Main Street in an hour? I want to talk to you, but this has to be it. Okay? I want us both to have closure here."

"Yes, okay! I'll meet you there." She half-smiled, half-cried as she got back into her VW Jetta and drove away.

I missed the Skype call, but immediately called Beth back from my cell. I'd never lied to her before, but for some reason I told her I was in a restaurant instead of at home. Part of it, I think, was because I wanted to keep the call short. Another part of me was embarrassed that without Beth in town, I had no plans on a Friday night.

It was super late on the East Coast and she sounded excited and maybe a bit anxious. She said the show went great and I was so happy to hear the news and, of course, to hear her sweet, high-strung voice. I was so happy she'd called, but hated the fact that I couldn't tell her everything about my day.

Then it hit me. I needed to go to New York. I needed to show her I meant everything I said and if it would take a huge gesture to get that point across, well then that was exactly what I was going to do. I told her I had to run and that I'd chat with her soon. Then, I immediately went online and found a last-minute deal to JFK. It was on a bit of a janky airline, but it was only 300 bucks and that couldn't be beat! I was going to make the grandest gesture and see if it would be enough. Since my flight was leaving at 7:00am, I jetted over to the pub with the intention of telling Laura I couldn't stay. I could have just called her, but she had come all this way and I wasn't about to hurt her the way she hurt me. It just wasn't my style. But when I got there and saw her beautiful face and wet eyes, I realized that I wasn't going to New York to find out if Beth loved me. I was going to prove to myself that I loved her more than I loved Laura. My what a tangled web we weave…

****

With the time difference, I got to JFK around 3:00pm. I hadn't thought far enough ahead to book a room, so I figured I'd just wander the city with my small backpack of boxers, t-shirts and toiletries until show time. Beth had posted a flyer on Instagram with the club address, so I knew where to find her. I was worried that even if I decided Beth was the right one for me, perhaps my simply showing up unannounced would freak her out. She had seemed so unsure when she left, and yet, she hadn't ended it. So something in her, if anything, was conflicted. How strange that I found that comforting!

Once I was reminded that New York was an extremely expensive city to get lost in, I sat up shop in a café around 5:00pm and messed around on my phone until it was time to go. I thought I'd be nervous, but I was instead calmed by the fact that I was going to have an answer, one way or another. For some reason, I felt compelled to email Riley and let her know my plan. If Beth was the one for me, I'd need an ally and Riley certainly was that. I asked that she not tell her sister I was there, so as not to ruin the surprise, and since I knew she was rooting for me, I figured she'd get it.

Maybe Beth would be mortified to see me! Maybe she'd be overjoyed. Maybe Laura would sense how pretty Beth is and call at the exact moment that I was touching her arm. But one thing was for certain: my heart was going to quiet down so that it could think straight. And if this had to happen during my girlfriend's all-women rock show, then that was where it would happen.

****

Okay, the nerves started to kick in a little once I got to the club. I had a beer at the bar. Then I had another. I looked around at the loud, fun-loving crowd and thought about the fact that each and every one of them had their own story. Maybe they all had lovers by their sides, but also ghosts who haunted them daily from their past. Maybe we were meant to love and pine for an unrequited or lost love simultaneously and that's just what everyone does. Or on the other hand, maybe I was just supposed to have another beer.

The show started and, as usual, Beth was incredible. She appeared confident and radiant and as lovely as ever, with just a little extra smattering of East Coast sass. The band sounded even better than before and it was clear they'd absolutely found their groove. I stayed in the back, in the shadows, as I didn't want to shake her nerves. At one point, I was sure she saw me as I noticed she got a bit nervous when her eyes met the crowd. I closed my eyes and listened to her sweet voice and wondered what the hell I was going to do.

After the final encore, the band disappeared into the back for a bit and I could feel my blood speeding up. It was like my arteries or blood vessels or whatever it is that's supposed to pump stuff to and from my ventricles had taken a caffeine pill. No amount of beer would slow it down. I couldn't believe I'd come to New York but I was excited that I did.

Then I saw her from across the room, still clad in a silly 80s outfit, still sweaty from the show. I watched as she glided through the crowd, her feminine brow furrowed as she searched. For what or whom she was searching, I didn't know, but I loved watching her glide.

She stepped right in front of me with her back turned and I could no longer wait. I touched her on the shoulder and she turned around.

Chapter Twenty-Nine:
A Beautiful Choice

Who would have thought that merely reigniting my life with a band audition could lead to so many new avenues? Here Nick was, standing directly in front of me in this random and strange city, with Jack finally so nearby. With one trip abroad, my world, which was once so tiny, like my cubicle at work or my circle of karaoke friends, had now expanded into a supernova. Or at least something close to it.

When Nick put his hand on my shoulder, I immediately recognized his touch. I turned around and acted surprised to see him, even though he's exactly who I was looking for. "Nick! What are you doing here? Have you been here the whole time?" I took his elbow and gently guided him into the greenroom. "Come with me, I can't hear you out here!"

"Surprise!" He pulled me in tightly and held me for a few sweet seconds. His backpack swung behind him, gently hitting me in the hip. "Oops sorry! I didn't know where to put this thing!" He awkwardly tilted his head and we stared at each other for a moment. Something was off. I knew it would be strange on my end, what with Jack somewhere in the next room, but it almost felt like Nick was disconnected, even though he'd come all this way.

He continued, "Do you want to go somewhere else to talk? Just you and me?"

I knew that I couldn't. I knew time was of the essence. "Not just yet. I need to stay around here for a bit. I'm so happy to see you, but I have to tell you that ..."

He stopped me in my tracks. "Beth, my ex, Laura, came to see me a while back. I didn't want to tell you because you had so much going on with the band. But, she wants to get back together. And of course, nothing happened. I would never do that. But I just had to tell you."

"So you flew to New York? You know I'm coming home in like a day, right? And there's the phone, and email and …"

"I love you. When I said that, I meant it and I still do. But I needed to tell you everything and it had to be in person this very moment. I needed to see if I felt what I think I feel. Or I don't know, I'm so confused."

Then it all became kind of funny in a kind of "Gift of the Magi" sort of way. "Nick, Jack is out there. I haven't talked to him yet, but he flew here from London. I didn't even want to speak to him until I told you. This is all so crazy." Then came the waterworks. "You have meant so much to me. You've changed my life and inspired me to become someone I really like."

"But you wanted to become that person for him, right? Not for me. It's okay, Beth, But let's be honest here."

"I don't know. I don't even know if I'll still have feelings for him once I see him. Maybe it was all just a dream, a fantasy. But whether I end up with him or someone else or no one, I think I was meant to have you in my life as a friend. And that's not me choosing Jack. It's just me, finally feeling clear about how I feel."

He cupped my chin with his soft hands. "I can't believe I'm going to say this. And truly, I'm amazed we're still standing here. That English guy is out there and you're sitting here talking to me? If ever the universe gave us our answers … this is it, kiddo. Yes, we'll be friends. Yes, it's okay. Maybe I'll end up with Laura, maybe not. But if you don't go out there and have some kind of dramatic kiss with that weirdo Englishman, I'm gonna do it for you. Unless he has bad teeth. Does he?"

"I want to kiss you right now but I fear that will give a conflicting message. So I will just say thank you, Nick. Thank you for coming all this way both to New York and into my life. Thank you for being my friend."

He smiled. "Go!" As I started to head out, he added. "Oh, do you know of any places I can crash? I kind of forgot to book a room." I started to think when he said, "Just kidding, go!"

I squeezed him for another hug and ran out of the green room and into the club, which was starting to thin out. I looked left, I looked right, I turned in a circle. Then I heard Jack's voice, which seemed as familiar to me as iced tea, say, "Hello love. Funny seeing you here." I turned toward him and literally fell into an embrace. I thought I might be shy, might not be able to speak when I was finally near him. But my body, or soul, or something other than the logical lobe of my mind took over and I found myself holding on to him for dear life. And even though I knew the story of what happened at the Tube station now, I also heard my voice exclaim, "Where did you go, Jack?! Where did you go?"

We both started to cry, which for me wasn't completely out of the norm. But for a buttoned-up Englishman, this was quite the spectacle. Stephen, who had been standing near us, muttered the words, "Oh blimey" as he walked toward the bar, presumably to get another pint.

"Where did I go?" he repeated. "I was just over there waiting for you."

I touched his sweater and smiled. "You're Jack, right? You're not your twin brother?"

He laughed heartily. "You'll never know, will you?"

But I knew it was Jack. I knew every ounce of him. His pheromones were undeniable and none of that had changed. "So what do we do now?"

"Well, for starters, we add each other on Facebook. I mean, whose bloody idea was it not to exchange mobile numbers? Or surnames? Beth Wilton!"

"This just isn't working out. We gave it our all, didn't we?"

He brushed a piece of my hair out of my eyes. "You funny American girl, you. I'm not letting you go that easily." He leaned in and kissed me so delicately I felt my ankles buckle. One hand held onto the back of my head, while the other clasped my hand and any doubt I had as to whether I was crazy or not, dissipated. "Would you like to get out of here and have a spot of tea or something?"

"I would love that, Jack Stoll. I would love that." We waved goodbye to Stephen, who smiled as we walked out of the club and onto the New York street. I didn't know what was going to be next and frankly, that was okay. "Oh and by the way, what in the heck was the name of that Beatles cover band?"

He laughed. "The Strawberry Fields? Why? Do you want to become a groupie?"

"No, I needed to know that. Just in case I lost you again."

He looked at me with a puzzled expression, shrugged, and then leaned in and kissed me. And with that, nothing in my life was ever small again.

THE END

www.ingramcontent.com/pod-product-compliance
Lightning Source LLC
Chambersburg PA
CBHW060648260626
47161CB00008B/3055